Carne's Raiders

By
Des Dunn

as
Sheldon B. Cole

First Published by Cleveland Publishing.

Republished in 2026 by Echo Books.

Echo Books is an imprint of Superscript Publishing Pty Ltd.
ABN 76 644 812 395.
Registered Office: 35 Keeley Lane, Princes Hill, Victoria, 3054.
www.echobooks.com.au

Copyright © Des Dunn Westerns Pty Ltd.
www.desdunnwesterns.com.au

Book Design: Jason McGregor.

ISBN: 978-1-923441-32-3 (Paperback)
ISBN: 978-1-922603-47-0 (ePub)

CHAPTER ONE
Worried Nights

Blake Durant was a man who made his own plans and went his own way, and his way for the moment was on the Sonora trail heading south. He wasn't looking for trouble, but he was ready for it, mainly because in the last three days of travelling he had come upon undeniable proof that some other people were bent on tearing the territory apart. Three days back, he had come upon a bullet-riddled ranch house, partially burned and deserted. A full hour's check had revealed nothing to him other than a woman had lived there with a husband and one child. This knowledge had been gained by washing left hanging on the back porch. The fact that the washing had been left behind told of a sudden, unplanned departure.

Then, two days ago, unable to pick up their trail and losing the tracks of about a dozen riders a mile to the south of the ranch house, he had come upon two graves set at the back of a clearing. There was nothing to give him a hint as to the identity of the two buried there. That afternoon he had heard shooting to the west of his own trail and the same night he'd been disturbed by the noisy approach of somebody from that sector. The somebody turned out to be a cowhand on foot, bleeding from four wounds. The cowhand had reeled past Blake and had fallen on his face. He was dead when Blake reached him.

After burying the cowhand, he had broken camp and gone on his way until three hours ago when, at sunup, he had come across a second ranch house which was also bullet-riddled and deserted.

Now, with the sun across his shoulders, he went along cautiously, instinctively knowing that sooner or later the trouble which was abundantly about him would come his way. The day was hot and windless and through the heat came the natural sounds of the terrain. Nothing more. It was a lonely day, like so many others he'd known in the last two years. On days like this, out on a trail which had no definite beginning or end, memories from the past usually plagued and tortured him. There were thoughts of the woman he had loved, of friends and relatives, of rolling cattle country that was still his but was the scene of too much sadness for him to return to it.

However, on this day he was spared these memories because the signs of violence and tragedy evoked a sense of danger that demanded his constant attention. As he rode along he looked carefully about him, missing nothing. Noon went by and the heat became almost insufferable. Durant worked his way closer to the valley side, seeking shade but finding none until he topped a long rise and discovered a smaller valley along whose sides were many boulders and a sprinkling of brush. Blake picked out a cluster of big rocks and rode his black stallion, Sundown, into their shade. He was coming out of the saddle, prepared to rest until day's end, when the thunder of hoofbeats broke the silence.

Blake's sharp eyes picked out the fast-moving, haze-blurred shapes of a group of riders. His hand dropped to his gun butt and he waited. But the riders swung together in a wide circle and went over the rim at the valley's end. Blake breathed a sigh of relief. Thoughts of the two burned-out ranch houses and the two graves were still with him.

He made a smokeless fire, boiled coffee and heated up beans. While he ate Sundown foraged for food. Studying the big black, Blake noticed that some of the sheen had gone from his coat. Sundown, powerful and strong-willed was, like his owner, in need of rest. The last few months had been strenuous for both of them. Hundreds of miles had been put behind in aimless drifting.

After putting out the fire, Durant stretched flat on his back and tried to sleep. But, despite the shade, the heat remained and sleep was denied him. He thought of the town ahead, and of the message he had for a man who lived there. The prospect of resting up for some days was pleasant.

Inevitably his thoughts again turned to home, where his younger brother was working their place. He saw Luke now in his mind's eye ... tall and slim, tough, dependable. He'd often tried to write to Luke. But what could he say?

Becoming restless, Blake went back into the saddle. Sage Creek should be about a half day's ride ahead, perhaps even closer. With three hours of daylight left, he decided to use them.

Putting Sundown into an easy trot, he came out of the shade and followed the trail left by the riders. Past the small valley the trail led through low hillsides thick with alder and birch and occasional firs. The country had benefited from recent rains, for the grass was thick and green in places. He found a rock pool and let Sundown drink, then he pushed on.

The sun was low on the horizon when Sundown climbed a rise. Blake reined up. Beneath him was a town set in a basin surrounded by small hills which seemed to lock it in. Blake liked the look of the place. He gave Sundown his head and the big stallion picked his way off the rise and stepped out eagerly to cross the well-grassed prairie.

Riding into the town's one street fifteen minutes later, Durant was pleased to learn that his distant approval of the place had plenty of foundation. The town had an air of prosperity about it which he hadn't noticed in any community for over a month. The stores were all freshly painted, and the houses had white fences, and gardens. The boardwalks lining the street were clean-swept. He immediately liked the place.

Slowing Sundown, he looked about for the business premises of Mort Field, saddler and gunsmith, for whom he had a letter written by Field's brother, Ambrose, Blake Durant's employer for a month. He had no idea what was in the letter.

It was in mid-town that he saw the sign creaking as it swung in the evening breeze. Hitching Sundown to the rack, Blake got down and worked the cramp out of his wide shoulders. He stood there for a moment, taking closer stock of the town, his approval of it deepening. Then he strode across the boardwalk, walked through the doorway and slopped before a bald-headed man who grunted as he stitched the side of a new saddle.

"Mr. Field?"

The man looked up. He had a weathered, kindly face.

"I'm Field," he said.

Blake pulled the letter from his pocket and gave it to him. "Your brother, Ambrose, asked me to deliver this."

Field accepted the letter eagerly, a smile creasing his face. He tore the envelope open, pulled out a single sheet of paper and unfolded it. He studied it heavily for a moment before his lips went thin. Then he passed the page to Durant, saying, "My eyes ain't so good these days, stranger. Would you do me the service of reading what Ambrose says?"

Blake studied the letter for a moment, his face brightening before he began to read:

"Mort, this here man is Blake Durant who is a good friend of mine. He'll tell you over some drinks I hope you'll buy for him that I'm fine and aim to stay that way. Got a new bull last fall and we had all the rain I need. Also, as you can see for yourself, I learned to write. I don't expect you've learned yet, so I don't hope for an answer to this. But maybe Durant will do you a favor, too, and put something down for you, then we'll both have written this year. Time's getting on, Mort, so when are you coming out? Best wishes from your brother, Ambrose, who wants to see you soon."

Blake handed the letter back to a beaming Mort Field. "Says that, eh, and he wrote it?"

"I saw him at it," Blake assured him.

Mort Field shook his head, as though he'd just witnessed a miracle. "Well, I declare, ain't that somethin' now, Ambrose sittin' and writin'." He looked at the letter again, then he folded it carefully and put it in his pocket. Looking soberly at Durant, he added, "I'm sure gonna start and learn to read, Mr. Durant, I sure am. Ambrose and me, we always promised each other that one day we'd do it. But what with one thing and another, I guess I never got round to it." He pushed the saddle away and dug the big needle into the wall, then he wiped his hands on his apron before taking it off. "Just rode in, eh?" he said.

Blake nodded.

"Then you can do with a drink and we can talk some. I was closin' up anyway with the light so bad. Will you wait a minute while I lock up?"

"Sure."

Mort Field hurried about the small store tending to the window locks before closing and putting a bar across the back door. He then washed his hands, smoothed the tufts of hair on each side of his bald head, and pulled a town coat from a peg on the wall. Coming to the front of the store, he motioned for Blake to go out. He was closing the door and chuckling to himself when a young woman came hurrying up the boardwalk.

Field and Blake Durant turned together as the woman stopped. Blake found himself looking into the face of one of the most beautiful young women he'd ever seen. Tall and slim, she was fetchingly dressed in a dark blue skirt and white silk blouse. Her long, dark hair was tied behind her head with a ribbon. Suddenly Blake realized he was staring. Her gaze went to him and her eyes narrowed. She turned to Field.

"Mr. Field, I must see you right away." Her voice was charged with emotion.

"Well, now, ma'am," Field said. "As you can see, I'm just closing up ..."

The woman moved closer to him and turned her back on Durant. But, although she lowered her voice and seemed determined to keep Blake out of the matter, he heard her say, "Mr. Field, it's very important. I meant to come earlier so as not to put you out, but I decided not to take any chances. Will you help me, please?"

Mort Field grunted thoughtfully, then nodded. To Durant he said, "You don't mind, do you?"

Blake, with the woman's challenging look fixed on him, shook his head. "I have lots of time."

Field pushed the door open and went inside. The young woman quickly followed and closed the door behind her, leaving Blake outside. But once again her attempt to confine the business between herself and Field didn't come off, for Durant could hear her plainly through the door.

"I want a gun, Mr. Field. And, please, I don't want any argument about it. It's your business to sell guns, isn't it? Well, I'm willing to pay any price."

Field said, "Now, hold on, ma'am. Sure, I sell guns and I don't much ask questions about why folks want one. Guess it's plain as the day itself why. But you being a woman and all and kind of upset to boot, I reckon maybe we should talk this out."

"No!" The sharp crack of that one word was followed by the clatter of something on the store counter. "This ring is worth a great deal more money than any gun could be, Mr. Field. I want to make a straight exchange, so you'll come out much better. Now, please, I don't want to argue anymore."

Blake opened the door and went in. But a board creaked under his weight and the young woman turned, her eyes bright with anger.

"What do you want?" she snapped.

"I overheard what was said, ma'am," Blake said easily. "Perhaps you should talk it out."

"And perhaps you should mind your own business," she said. "I'm not breaking any law."

"A gun is a right handy piece of hardware for defending yourself," Blake went on, ignoring her bitterness. "But in your case it strikes me that defense isn't the position. People get hurt taking up a gun, and some get themselves killed."

8

"Don't interfere!" she exploded, her face white with anger. She glared at him until her lips quivered and her hands trembled. Then her face grew tight and tears welled in her eyes. Her trembling became worse until she seemed to have lost control of herself, then Mort Field said quietly:

"Mr. Durant is a friend of my brother's, ma'am. You can see by the look of him and his manner, that he ain't no man to leave a woman out on a limb. Also, seeing as how something has hit you real hard, maybe you know enough about me to trust me. And maybe we can be of service, ma'am."

The young woman looked at each of them in turn, then the tears overflowed and streaked down her cheeks. Her body swayed and Durant reached out to steady her. She tried to jerk free of his grip, but he merely held her stare and shook his head.

"The situation may not be as impossible as you think," he said.

Her gaze held his and suddenly her crying stopped. She bit at her bottom lip and took a deep breath as though to get full control of herself. Then, in a voice Blake Durant could scarcely hear, she said:

"There's nothing left for me to do but what I must. Nothing at all."

Field had moved off.

He came back with a chair and she sat down. Then Field picked up her ring from the counter and put it on her finger. When she looked up, startled, Field said:

"I ain't about to take the last valuable thing a woman has, ma'am, which is what I figure that ring is. Also, it could be that it means a lot to you. Now, I'll fetch a brandy and you can do some thinking and then maybe some talking. Later, if Durant and me can see no way of stopping you or helping you, you'll have your gun."

The young woman folded her hands on her lap and stared down at them. Blake sensed that her thoughts were far away from this room. And he guessed now that whatever had driven her to come here for a gun didn't seem quite as important to her now. It was almost as if her fight had ended and she had accepted defeat. Field brought the brandy. After refusing it with a shake of her head, she finally took the glass and drank the brandy down, shuddering as the liquor burned her throat.

"Thank you," she said a moment later to Mort Field, and color gradually returned to her face. Blake Durant studied her closely and guessed her age to be in the late twenties. She had a refined look about her, yet it was obvious that her hands were not strangers to hard work. She could be a married woman who'd had the grit to give up an easy life to pull her weight with a man trying to make something of himself. But there was nothing matronly about her to suggest that she had reared a family.

"Might be a help if we knew your name," Field said to her.

Blake saw her hands clench tightly. Then she said, "My name is Beth Matheson. My husband was Paul Matheson."

"Was?" Field said. "Paul Matheson. Hell, I know him. I saw him in town only a few days ago—last weekend, I think it was."

"He's dead now," Beth Matheson said in a monotone, as if all feeling had left her.

Field said, "Paul didn't strike me as the kind that'd just up and die."

"He didn't, Mr. Field. He was killed, murdered. I saw it. I saw the man who shot him down just as I saw my nephew killed when the others came." Tears were running down her cheeks again and her bosom heaved under the stress of recalling the tragedy. "I saw him as plain as I'm seeing you now, Mr. Field. It was Tom Carne."

"Carne!" The name exploded from Field. Blake fixed him with a questioning look and Field said. "Gun hand. Rides, tall in these parts, as wild as they come. He's the kind who kills and doesn't even blink."

Blake returned his attention to the young woman and found her eyes focused on him. He said, "If you know all this, why not go to the law, Mrs. Matheson? Looking for revenge against that kind isn't a smart thing to do."

"The law?" she said, her voice edged with contempt. "You must be a stranger to these parts, Mr. Durant. The law here is Sheriff Horrie Sylvester. I think Mr. Field will agree that he's as despicable a man as Carne."

Blake turned to Mort Field who shrugged and said, "Sylvester ain't exactly no angel, Durant. There's been plenty of bad talk about him."

"Do you have any friends in this town?" Blake asked.

"I thought I did have, Mr. Durant," she replied, her voice steady now. "And I went to them. There were men who visited my husband from time to time. Sometimes he rode off with them, supposedly to drive cattle or some other business. They were always rewarding trips for Paul, sometimes so rewarding that I should have become suspicious a long time ago. But I loved him, you see, and a woman blinded by love is blind to everything."

Field appeared about to interrupt, but Durant motioned for him to be quiet. Beth Matheson fidgeted with her blouse string for a moment, then smiled without humor. Looking up, she said, "My husband was an outlaw, Mr. Durant. Finally the truth of that was too obvious to be ignored. We talked about it and I made Paul see that his past was bad. He promised me to change his ways, and he held to his word for over three months. He never went with that crowd again. But then, a few nights ago, Tom Carne rode up and Paul was nervous. Carne hurried him outside to the porch and closed the door in my face. I heard them arguing and then a gun went off.

When I ran out to them, Carne was standing there with a gun in his hand and smoke was rising between him and Paul, who was clutching at his stomach. Then my nephew, who'd been visiting us, rushed out. Carne jumped off the porch and a number of men rode up in the darkness. I was so shocked and distraught I didn't know what was happening. Bullets were coming from everywhere. Then I heard my nephew scream in pain and saw him staggering across the clearing. By the time I got to him, somebody had fired the porch with a tar stick and then somebody else rode over me and I was kicked in the head by a hoof. Luckily it was only a glancing blow. When I came to, the house had been burned down and my nephew and my husband were dead."

Beth Matheson sat there, stiff-shouldered, her lips compressed, her face vacant.

Blake Durant stepped back from her, his face devoid of expression. He remembered the first ranch house he had passed, and later the two graves. The graves had been at least a mile from the ranch house.

He said, "Why did you take their bodies away from that place, Mrs. Matheson?"

Beth jerked her head up and anger filled her eyes again. "To show people, that's why. I was going to bring their bodies to town. I wanted everybody to know what a murdering snake Tom Carne is!"

"Why did you change your mind on the way?"

"I realized how hopeless it was, Mr. Durant. Knowing the kind of man Sheriff Sylvester is, I saw I could expect no help from him. And there was another reason. If I was going to do something about it, it would be better to come into town alone and unseen. So I came here to see Ed Woodrow and Ty Pullen, who often visited Paul. Although they'd had nothing to do with me, they struck me as being on friendly terms with Paul. So I offered them money, everything we had saved."

Looking at the ring she had tried to exchange for a gun, Blake said, "And they took it?"

Beth smiled bitterly and nodded. "Oh, yes, they took it all, and they said they'd do what they could about Carne. That was two days ago. I've seen Tom Carne a few times since—and I've seen them, too, always drinking. I approached Ed Woodrow only this afternoon and he laughed in my face and told me to wake up to myself. Pullen laughed, too, and I realized then what a fool I'd been. Pullen and Woodrow are actually friends of Tom Carne's, or at least they're frightened of him."

Blake had the full picture now, and his heart went out to this gritty woman. But what could he do to help her get the vengeance she sought?

"You won't need that gun," he told her firmly. "What I want you to do is go someplace and rest. Leave this to me. I don't know what I can do yet, but I'll be working on it."

Beth rose shakily to her feet and smoothed down her skirt. Then she glanced from Field to Durant and back again, doubt and surprise in her eyes.

"But why?" she asked.

Blake shrugged. Then he asked, "How much did you pay them?"

"Four hundred dollars, Mr. Durant."

Blake walked to the door, opened it and looked into the night. Sundown was standing quietly at the hitchrail, patiently waiting to be stalled and fed. Blake turned.

"Mr. Field, will you take care of Mrs. Matheson? Keep her out of the way?"

"I sure will, Durant." Field paused. "Look, before you go off half-cocked, for hell's sake, listen to me. You don't know what in blazes you're letting yourself in for. That outfit's so rotten and—"

Mort Field cut himself off, for the doorway was empty. A moment later came the sounds made by a walking horse. He hurried to the boardwalk with the woman behind him and saw the big drifter astride Sundown. The big man was soon swallowed up by the darkness.

"Well, ma'am, that's that for the moment," Field said. He looked into her eyes. "I just hope you've got the sense to keep out of this. You butt in and you might make it worse. You got yourself a room in town?"

"At the rooming house, Mr. Field."

"I'll take you there, get you some grub, then I want you to hit the hay. All right by you?"

Beth didn't reply. She kept looking into the darkness into which Blake Durant had gone. Somehow it seemed natural that he should help her. She wondered how it would have been if she'd met a man like him when she was younger. Paul Matheson had turned her head with his fancy manners, fine talk and big ambitions. Even on the night she had accepted his proposal of marriage, she'd had her doubts. But then she'd decided that all young women had these doubts when making the biggest decision of their lives.

She turned her wedding ring around on her finger as she went along the boardwalk with Mort Field.

CHAPTER TWO

The Gun Packers

Blake Durant pushed open the batwings and hesitated, hands holding the doors still. His stare travelled over the crowded saloon and settled on the noisiest group, a crowd of some ten men packed into the far corner. Two, their faces whisky-flushed, were jostling each other and bumping into the others, but nobody seemed to care. They were big men, cumbersome in their movements.

Blake entered the room and took a position at the bar from where he could watch the noisy group and at the same time see all the other customers. The barkeep served him a rye and brought back his change. Blake wanted to ask some questions but he held his tongue. There was plenty of time, he decided, if Field could just keep the Matheson woman quiet and out of things.

After his second drink he felt some of the weariness leave his body. His mind seemed clearer, too, and he wondered how often he could become a fool like this before somebody shot him dead. Not that gunfighting bothered him much these days. Being a loner, he had learned to suffer suspicion and stand his ground against crowding. It was almost always the same—the questions, the looks, and finally the attempt to make him accept the fact that he was no more than a drifter. Why people wouldn't let well enough alone, he had not yet come to understand. But he had learned to expect their interference.

The barkeep was cleaning the counter nearby when Blake decided the time had come for more positive action. He knew nothing about this town except that the sheriff was a man of dubious reputation and that a man named Tom Carne did more or less as he liked. It added up to an unhealthy situation in a town that seemed so pleasant.

"Do you know a man named Pullen, or one named Woodrow?" he asked the barkeep, then he watched the man's gaze harden at the mention of the names.

"Yeah, I know 'em, stranger."

"Are they here now?"

"You hear that noise, mister? Follow it and you'll find them sure enough."

It was just as Blake had guessed—a hellion crew letting down their hair, enjoying the fruits of cheating a woman out of her money and expecting no repercussions on the matter. He glanced past the shoulders of a group of townsmen and saw the ten men still jostling about, pulling a whisky bottle from each other's hands and spilling more than they drank. He carefully weighed up the men in the group, finally deciding that they looked no more dangerous than any other men who rode in a mob.

"Obliged," he told the barkeep before ordering a bottle of whisky. He paid for it and walked along the bar. Stopping just short of the group, he uncorked the bottle. Taking a good-sized drink, he wiped his mouth on his sleeve, and then, conscious that he had gained the attention of some of the group, he asked:

"Pullen here, or Woodrow?"

In a blink the crowd stopped wrestling for the bottle of whisky and Blake took another drink.

"Who wants to know?" somebody asked.

"I'm Blake Durant, up from the Platte country," Blake told the cowhand on his left, a runt with a scarred jaw and eyes so close together he seemed to have no bridge to his nose. Blake offered him the bottle but the runt shook his head.

Blake gave a barely perceptible shrug and pulled the bottle back when another man stepped in front of him. He was tall and lean and he smelled of stale whisky and tobacco smoke. His mouth was tight and though he might have once been a handsome man, the hardness of his features had ruined the promise of this a long time ago.

"What do you want with Ed Woodrow?" he asked in a surly voice.

Blake held his look evenly, noticing that the others had drawn back, leaving one of the mob to stand on his own. Every eye studied him sourly and he knew that one false step would mean trouble for him—trouble he mightn't be able to handle if he didn't take the initiative.

"I rode a long way to talk to him," Blake said. "We have mutual friends along the Platte and I'm at a loss in this town."

"The Platte?" The tall man began to shake his head. "No, I don't recollect havin' any friends down that way, Durant. Maybe you should give out some other names and—"

Blake threw the bottle to the runt and grabbed Woodrow by the shirt front. His gun appeared in his hand and he rammed the muzzle against the man's grimy neck. At the same time he took two steps back and planted his spine against the counter. Then he turned Woodrow around, by twisting his arm behind his back, and he said, "Now, where's Pullen?"

The gun hands remained immobile while their befuddled minds tried to determine the best move to make. Blake saw three of them throw nervous glances in the direction of another man who was separated, as if by personal choice, from the others.

Blake said to the lone man, "Okay, mister, you'll do for Pullen. Turn and walk, slow, then open the back door and go out. Try to run and your friend here gets it."

The ugly man he spoke to was burly and thick-necked. His arms, huge and hairy, swung at his sides. He didn't move, nor did any of the others. Behind Blake a deep silence had settled.

"You have ten seconds to make up your mind, mister," Blake told the man he suspected was Pullen. "After that I'll start crowding a little more."

Woodrow began to turn but the pressure of the gun against his neck suddenly increased, making him stiffen.

The other said, "You can go to hell, Durant."

"If I do, mister, at least two of you will go with me. Make up your mind."

For a moment Blake saw uncertainty in Pullen's rough-hewn face. He shoved Woodrow away, but he was quick to follow him and keep the gun hard against his neck. Moving his captive about in a circle, he managed to draw away from the group and towards the back door. Pullen turned as Woodrow and Durant did, and his hand began to edge towards his gun. Blake noticed that a few of the others had finally decided to buy into the fight.

He said, "At a time like this, gents, whoever makes the first move is the first dead. Think hard. All I want is Woodrow and Pullen who, up to date, have proved themselves a match only for womenfolk."

Woodrow's mouth gaped and Pullen frowned. It was Pullen who rasped, "What damned woman are you talking about, Durant? What the hell is this, anyway?"

"I've come to collect four hundred dollars, Pullen," Blake said. "And I think I've got a better chance of getting it out of your pockets outside than in here. You have your last chance to move."

Blake Durant snagged back the hammer of his gun. Pullen licked at his lips and then he looked nervously around. Nobody at the bar had attempted to buy in.

Durant reached the doorway and told Woodrow to open it. When the gun hand did so, Blake levelled the gun on Pullen. For just a moment Woodrow evidently felt he had a chance to escape and he lunged forward. But Blake put out a boot and tripped him. Then, as Pullen steeled himself to dive forward, Blake grabbed Woodrow by the shirt, dragged him to his feet and hammered him against the side of the doorway. The gun hand let out a howl of pain and his face went white. Blake put his gun against the man's lips and watched the sweat fall.

"Ty, for hell's sake," Woodrow said. "Do like he says. He's loco."

Ty Pullen raised his hand from his gun butt. His glance at Ed Woodrow told everybody there that a friendship was at an end. Blake Durant read this from the man's look and kept his gun trained on the bigger man. When Pullen came slowly towards him, he didn't allow himself a moment of relaxation. He knew things could still happen, that somebody could be killed. He didn't want that. All he wanted was to get Beth's money. Then she could go to another town where a trusted lawman could look into her allegations. He felt he was halfway towards achieving that aim.

Then Pullen walked past him. Blake stepped back, giving him no chance to grab at his gun. A killing now might set things into motion. Against ten men, he'd have little chance.

Pullen moved into the yard. Blake pushed Woodrow forward and covered them both. He didn't bother to close the back door of the saloon. Motioning both gun hands to continue towards the saloon laneway, he was careful to keep them in the light and himself out of it. He heard footsteps inside the saloon and saw a shadow fill the doorway. But the man evidently thought better of his action and jumped back.

Blake forced Woodrow and Pullen to the fence, made them stand in the light and ordered them to empty their pockets. Woodrow was quick to comply, handing over a bundle of crumpled bills and cursing under his breath. Blake pushed him back against the fence and turned to Pullen.

"Mister, all I want is that widow's money. Later on somebody else will settle with your friend, Tom Carne, for murder, but as far as I'm concerned, that's another matter. Empty your pockets and quick."

Pullen's hands went into his pockets. He pulled out a roll of bills that he tossed onto the ground. Then, his lips curling back in a snarl of contempt, he said, "Bend for it, drifter."

Blake ignored the money, knowing what Pullen had in mind. He reached out and pulled Pullen forward, then he drove his gun-loaded fist into the big man's stomach. When Pullen folded over, groaning, Blake brought the gun down and onto the side of the gun hawk's head. Pullen fell without a sound. Blake then motioned for Woodrow to pick up the money. When he had it in his hand, he shoved it into his pocket and stepped away from Woodrow.

Blake said, "Stay put for five minutes, mister. Move and I might be close enough to shoot your guts out. And when your friend wakes up, tell him to leave Mrs. Matheson alone. The same goes for you."

Woodrow just stared. Blake edged silently into the dark, then he went down the laneway and headed for the other end of town.

* * *

The little man leaned forward and slapped Woodrow hard, twice, across the face. A trickle of blood ran from Woodrow's mouth. It was no surprise to any watching to see Woodrow take the attack and do nothing about it. They all knew, as Woodrow did, that once anger fired Tom Carne, somebody could be killed.

"You let one man, a stinkin' drifter, come in and kick the feet out from under you, mister?" the little man growled.

Carne turned and studied the other men. Ty Pullen was absent, having the side of his head attended to by the town doctor.

"Nobody, not a damned one of you, lifted a hand to stop him. Isn't that right?"

Nobody answered. The Carne bunch had the saloon to themselves. On Carne's orders, the barkeep had left ten minutes ago. Sheriff Horrie Sylvester had called in and had then gone on his way, leaving the matter of Durant to Carne for the moment.

Carne glared ferociously at Woodrow again. "We got
a town in the palms of our hands. We got all the outlying
country for the taking. There's one trail in and one trail out—
unless some fool tries to cross the mountains in this kind of
weather. So what do I find?"

Carne motioned for Woodrow to pour him a drink. When
he had it, he sipped it lightly and rolled the whisky around
in his small mouth. He stared at the table, deep in thought,
before going on.

"I find that I've hired me a bunch of fools who are cowards
to boot. One damned man, a drifter, comes in and bucks the
whole set-up." Carne's evil little eyes went to each man in
turn. Then he suddenly hurled the glass down at the table
top and roared, "Find Durant! Get Durant for me! Get him
inside of an hour! Move!"

Carne reached out and began shoving men in all
directions. Then he lashed out at the whisky bottle and sent it
shattering against the wall near Woodrow. Woodrow let out a
howl and jumped back. Carne closed in on him, drew his gun
and used it to beat him to the floor. The others hurried for
the exits. When all had gone, Tom Carne stared down at the
bloodied face of Woodrow. Speaking very quietly, he said,
"Ed, find Durant for me. Hurry now!"

Carne helped his hireling from the floor and pushed him
on his way. Woodrow, dazed and hurt, stumbled about,
banging into other tables before he groped his way along the
counter and all but fell through the batwings.

Tom Carne stood there, eyes closed, breathing in deeply as he tried to arrest the anger which consumed him. Never before had he allowed any man to buck him. He had, when starting on his plan to take over the town and the surrounding country, hand-picked the men he needed to help him. In two instances now they had failed him. The first had been at the Matheson place when he had almost been shot down by a brat bursting from the ranch house, and the second time was this night, when a drifter nobody had heard of had coolly walked in and cut his men down to size. Knowing full well how much his success depended on cowing the townspeople, he couldn't stomach this failure tonight. Durant would have to be found and an example had to be made of him.

He walked across to the bar and pulled a fresh bottle from under the counter. Pulling off the cork, he lifted the bottle to his lips and drank greedily. Whisky spilled down his chin and neck and soaked into his shirt. He kept at it until he felt his throat contracting, then he slid the bottle down the counter, pulled out his gun and walked from the saloon.

Sheriff Horrie Sylvester, who had been watching and listening since leaving the saloon earlier, showed himself in the glow of the street light. Carne looked bleakly at him for a moment before he growled:

"Horrie, we've got to spill some blood. It's been a long time since something like that happened. Folks hereabouts are maybe getting the idea that the worst is past and we can be checked."

Sylvester shook his head. "Nope, Tom, ain't anybody about to think that way, not as I see it."

"What you see ain't what I see. This Durant, you know him at all?"

"Never heard of him."

"You ain't checked?"

"Sure I checked, Tom. He rode in, paid a call on old Mort Field and then he showed up in the saloon."

"Field," Carne said, and the cold way he said the name sent a shiver through Horrie Sylvester. From the beginning Sylvester had been more than willing to throw in with Carne. Most of his life had been spent taking orders from older lawmen. He'd spent years doing all the hard chores and getting little thanks for it. But now, under Carne, he was somebody. The town was afraid of him. But he still retained some sense of proportion and he felt he knew just how far people could be pushed. Tom Carne didn't seem to give a damn about taking precautions.

"Mort Field is one of the best liked people in this town," Sylvester said. "Also, he's an old man who can't do much harm to anybody."

"He can scheme, Horrie, and he can talk. So what you do is take care of him. Tonight."

The color drained from Sylvester's face. He had no fear of Mort Field and he had no doubt that he could easily put the old buzzard out of the way. But people were already talking about what Durant, a stranger, had done that evening, and some of them knew that Durant had visited Field. He had even heard it mentioned that Beth Matheson had called on Field.

"Hell, Tom," he said, "if you have old Mort put out of the way, then a lot of people are sure to—"

Carne moved a step forward and suddenly his gun appeared in his hand. His eyes were glazed; he looked crazy. Sylvester shifted nervously and sucked in a quick breath, holding out both hands, palms up.

"Okay, okay, Tom," he said. "Whatever you say."

"Tonight, Horrie. In the morning one of you is gonna be dead, either you or him."

Tom Carne turned and walked away. Watching him go, Horrie Sylvester had the fleeting wish to draw and shoot him down. But he didn't have enough confidence in himself, not even when looking at Carne's back. He had heard too much about Carne's gun handling ability. So he went on his way, resigned to killing an old man he felt no bitterness for.

CHAPTER THREE
Death Has No Vacation

Mort Field, after having sent a tray of food to Beth Matheson at the rooming house, didn't know what to do with himself. He was worried about Durant, a man he respected and liked. Durant had struck him as a man who kept to himself and minded his own business, but there was something in him that wouldn't allow him to walk away from a woman in trouble. Mort had met a lot of men like that in his time. Even the craggiest and roughest of Mort's friends in the old days, and there had been plenty of them, couldn't stomach seeing a defenseless woman abused. But things were different now; men were afraid.

Mort Field ate at the main street cafe. Then, passing up his usual two drinks at the saloon, he returned to his shop to wait for news about Durant. Sitting at his bench and working on the saddle stitching again, he turned his thoughts to the other problems which had been worrying him for so long. He had felt for some time now that something should be done about Carne and his hellion outfit. But Carne was all-powerful. He was a killer, and had proved it by shooting five men who had attempted to stop his activities. He had first of all installed himself in the saloon. He was always on hand when trouble erupted and he never failed to put an end to it.

He told himself that one day somebody would bring Carne down to size. Until that day came, Mort could see no way to fight the killer. Sheriff Horrie Sylvester was another thing. Sylvester, in his year's reign as town lawman, had done little before Tom Carne arrived in town.

He'd arrested drunks, stopped a couple of street brawls, sent a crowd of rough-riding Texas cattlemen on their way, but in the main he loitered about, taking his drinks whenever he wanted them and seldom paying. But, with the advent of Tom Carne, Horrie Sylvester had grown a couple of inches and now he walked with a swagger. Of course, Carne had Sylvester in the palm of his hand, Mort Field had no doubt at all. But what could anybody do about that? Neither Carne nor Sylvester had done anything illegal.

Not until now, Mort thought. Beth Matheson's story was a shocking revelation about Carne's ambition. The fact that Beth Matheson's husband, Paul, had been proved one of Carne's mob hardly surprised Mort. Paul had never impressed Mort Field much, in fact so little that he wondered what a woman like Beth Matheson had seen in him.

Mort went on with his stitching and thinking. As far as he knew, there were enough decent and courageous men in this town to handle scum like Carne, but perhaps only after a bloody business which none wanted to get involved in.

Mort Field, after an hour's work, found his fingers beginning to ache. He realized he was getting old. He could remember sitting up all day and half the night making saddles or repairing guns. But now, after only a couple of hours at his work, he found his back hurting and his fingers aching. He put the needle away, stood up and stretched his arms. If it hadn't been for Durant and the Matheson woman, he would have gone to bed in his quarters out back.

But on this night he knew sleep would not come to him, although he had heard no noise from the saloon at all since going to his shop.

He walked through the shop to his living quarters, and got the pot-bellied stove going. Standing there and watching the flames lick out, he felt no loneliness at all. He hadn't been lonely one day of his life, mainly because he always kept his mind and his hands busy. He knew that was the secret of happiness and he wondered why other people didn't see it. Durant, now, he decided, was a lonely man. There was a graveness in his face, the absence of a smile, the careful way his eyes looked at you and took you in and missed nothing. Durant was big and strong and young, and Mort wondered why he hadn't taken up with a woman like Beth Matheson. Putting his coffee pot on to boil, he stood by the stove rubbing his hands together. He wasn't cold, but the heat seemed to take the stiffness out of his hands.

Finally the coffee boiled. He poured himself a mugful and was sitting on the edge of his bunk, sipping, when he heard a scratch of sound in the yard. Despite his age, his hearing was as good as it had ever been. He liked to say that on still nights he could hear a bug scratching.

Putting down his coffee mug, Mort Field made his way to the back door. He stood against the wall and pressed his ear against the old timber. There was silence in the yard now, broken only by the gentle wash of the wind through the flowering bushes he'd so carefully cultivated.

Five minutes passed and Mort Field, exhibiting the patience of a man who had hunted all his life, remained absolutely still. The wind was the only sound outside. Beginning to believe that he must have been mistaken, Mort released the catch on the back door and pulled the door towards him. The darkness was so deep that it took him several seconds to make out even the line of the bushes and the fence beyond them. His gaze swept around for several moments before, with a shrug, he began to pull the door closed. It was then that Horrie Sylvester, whose patience was at breaking point, put his shoulder to the door on the run and slammed Mort back inside. Mort lost his footing under the impact of the lean man's charge and fell. But the moment he hit the floor he lashed out with his boots for a hold and got his hands under him.

He was in the act of rising when Sylvester, gun in hand, closed the door and pushed the catch home. Sylvester planted his back against the timber and looked down at the old man. There was not one vestige of fear in Mort's age-seamed face.

"Okay, on your feet and mind your manners, Field. I came to have a chat with you and you best come up with the right answers to what I ask you."

Mort glared at Sylvester as he got to his feet, in no way hurt by the fall.

"What the hell do you want, Sylvester? You come to rob an old man? Not gettin' enough handouts in town?"

Sylvester looked about the room, unnecessarily, because during his waiting outside he had discovered that Field was alone. But he always liked to be dead certain. It was this cautious approach in all his dealings with people that had saved his life more than once.

"What the hell do you want?" Field demanded.

Sylvester waved his gun. "I'll ask the questions. And mind how you talk to me. Now what's with you and Durant?"

"Who?"

"The drifter who rode in at sundown and went straight to you. Don't lie to me—I ain't in any mood to be bandied about with."

Mort Field shook his head innocently. "Sylvester, I get a lot of people come to my shop. Some want saddles repaired, some want to buy a new one. Sometimes it's bridles or saddlebags or the like. And sometimes it's a gun."

"I know all about your lousy business, Field," Sylvester said angrily. It was always the same with old people, he thought. They were so damned sure of themselves and hardly ever frightened. It was almost as if they'd decided death was inevitable and the sooner the better.

Sylvester jerked his gun up as Mort Field went to the pot-bellied stove and poured himself a mug of coffee.

Boiling inside, Sylvester growled: "Durant stayed for a good while in your shop, mister. When he came out you were with him. You were seen by a friend of mine whose job it is to check out every new face in town, day or night. So Durant ain't just a customer."

Mort Field smiled at the lawman. "Sylvester, I think maybe you've been totin' tin too long. You're nervous, mister, and in that state a lawman is likely to come apart at the seams. But, if it helps you any, Durant saw me working and came in to ask where to stay in town and for advice on where to look for a job."

Sylvester's lips peeled back scornfully. "A damned lie! What about the woman, the Matheson woman?"

"What about her?" Field asked, realizing that his bluff might at any moment be exposed. If Sylvester had in fact been informed by somebody about the talk on the boardwalk outside his shop, or even inside it, he knew he could be in great trouble.

"She came at a rush into your place and then Durant followed her and you in. When you all came out later, she went off with you and Durant headed for the saloon. None of that would worry me ordinarily, Field, but what happened later sure does."

"Like what?" Field asked.

"Like Durant frontin' Pullen and Woodrow and then takin' 'em outside the saloon and robbin' them."

"He did that?" Mort Field said, unable to keep a rise of excitement out of his voice.

"Yeah, mister, that's what he did. Then he ran off into the dark. But not before he mentioned working for the Matheson woman, who visited you and was seen talking with Durant and you."

Sylvester came slowly away from the door and Mort Field took a firmer hold on his coffee mug. He regretted that the coffee had cooled down some and would not, in the event of trouble, be a potent enough weapon against Sylvester's gun. He felt tension rising inside him, but no fear. Sylvester's kind, with their bullying, had never worried him in the whole of his life.

"Y'know what?" Sylvester said. "I got to thinking that Durant aimed to take up the woman's problems, and you helped. You know where that puts you in this town, don't you?"

"Where, Sylvester?"

Sylvester grabbed him by the shirt and attempted to drag him forward. Field's reaction was to hurl the coffee into his face. Sylvester spluttered but the coffee was only lukewarm, so he reached out again. But Field had grabbed the coffee pot. Now wheeling around with surprising agility for an old man, he let fly with the pot. It glanced off the side of Sylvester's head and sent him reeling.

Mort Field made a dash for the curtained doorway leading into his shop, but Sylvester punched off a shot. The bullet took Field in the middle of the back and he was thrown forward with such impact that he went into the corridor, pulling the curtains and their rod down over himself. He didn't move.

Sylvester, cursing, hurried across to him and dragged him by the legs back into the light. But when he turned him over and saw the blood on his chest from the exit hole, he knew the old man was dead. He drew back, ready to make a run for it, when he saw the edge of a slip of paper sticking out of Mort Field's pocket. He pulled it clear, unfolded it and read quickly.

A thin smile pushed the nervousness out of his face, then he pocketed the letter from Ambrose Field and hurried to the back door. Drawing back the catch, he opened the door and peered nervously out into the yard.

Damn Field! he told himself. And damn Tom Carne, too!

Horrie Sylvester hated being in a position like this, not knowing who was watching or who was close by. Then he rushed into the yard, sank down on his knees in the darkness near Field's bushes and after a long, tense minute, rose and made his way silently across the yard and over the fence.

Then he waited again, just to make sure, and when nobody came to check on the shot, he went off, mopping at his brow.

* * *

Blake Durant visited the livery stable as soon as he left the saloon. He found Sundown standing in the front yard with two other horses. Calling him, he opened the gate and the big black came out. Then he roused the stable attendant and got his saddle. The two hours' rest seemed to have freshened Sundown enough, Durant thought, to enable the big black to make a short run from town. Then, with the night to rest up in, he was sure the black would be his old self by morning. Taking Sundown into the alleyway behind Field's place, he left the horse there and proceeded towards the rooming house. An enquiry at the foyer desk established the fact that Beth Matheson was booked into room fourteen. Getting directions from the hawk-nosed clerk, Blake climbed the steps, located the room at the end of a long passageway and rapped lightly on the door.

"Who is it?" came Beth's nervous voice.

Durant said, "I have your money, Mrs. Matheson."

He heard the key turn on the inside, then the door opened. Beth Matheson was still fully dressed and her bag was on the bed, closed. Blake handed her the money, saying, "I don't know how much is there, and I didn't have time to collect any that might be missing."

Beth took the money and didn't bother to count it. Looking straight at him, puzzled a little, she said, "It's not the money that counts."

"For the moment it's the best we can do, Mrs. Matheson. I've created quite a stir in town and I expect trouble tonight. I think it would be better if you slept somewhere else."

Beth frowned at him. "What did you do, Mr. Durant?"

"I had a talk with a couple of your acquaintances. I don't think they appreciated my demanding the return of your money. No matter. I see you've packed, so let's go."

Beth looked anxiously at him as she stepped back a pace. She hesitated, unsure of herself. "Where can I go?" she asked.

"We'll find a place. The important thing right now is not to waste time—unless you want a bunch of gun rannies bursting in looking for me. They know I acted on your behalf."

Beth still frowned at him. Then, when Durant turned away, she hurried to the bed and picked up her bag. In the doorway, Durant took the bag from her and saying no more led the way out of the passageway. This time he left the rooming house via the rear door. As he waited to check out the yard, he smelled the sweet scent of her close behind him. Her freshness excited him and he glanced across at her to find her looking at him.

He said, "I think it will work out all right, Mrs. Matheson, provided that for the moment you do exactly as I say."

"But where are we going? I can't just walk off with you into the night. I'm a married woman, or at least, I was."

"You need have no worry on that score, ma'am," Durant said as he led the way across the yard. When they reached the side laneway, Sundown snorted a welcome. Blake tied the bag to his saddle and asked, "Do you have a horse, Mrs. Matheson?"

She nodded. Somehow the darkness made Blake look taller and more mysterious. But she sensed that questioning him further would be to no avail.

"My horse is at the stables," she said.

"In your name?"

"Yes."

"Then wait here."

Durant went off and returned five minutes later leading her horse. He was relieved to find it was a big, sturdy animal, suitable for the ride they had ahead of them. After checking the saddle girth, he told her to mount up and was impressed by the way she climbed into the saddle without his help. Rubbing Sundown's nose, he turned and looked into the darkness again.

"You'll be all right here, Mrs. Matheson. If somebody comes, draw back against the fence. There's plenty of room for somebody to pass and you won't be seen against the fence."

"Where are you going now?" she asked. "And what do you have in mind?"

"I have to check back with Field and tell him what I'm up to. I won't be long."

Beth had her mouth open to protest, but Blake slipped into the darkness and she found herself alone. The dark had never worried her before, not even when Paul had been away and she was alone on their place. In fact, she had often walked at night. But now, sitting her horse in the dark, she was frightened. So much had happened to her lately. So much pain had come into her life. She thought of her nephew, no more than a boy, but showing a man's courage when he had without hesitation gone after Tom Carne. But he couldn't, of course, match the viciousness and cunning of the killer. She knew she would never forget him, nor would she cease to mourn his going.

The night was cool and absolutely silent about her, and she jumped in fright when she felt something cold against her hand. But then she saw the big head of the stranger's horse lifted towards her and she patted it. The horse, like the man, was powerful. When that thought entered her head, Beth began to think of the man again. She was curious how he had managed to get her money back from the two hellions, who were, she had discovered that very day, always in the company of Tom Carne's rotten breed.

Blake Durant was quite a man. She did not know him, yet she had trusted him.

This was not like her; she had always been a careful woman, trusting very few people since her mother and father had been duped out of their ranch in Montana so many years ago.

The memory of that still hurt her, not so much because of the loss of property but more because the theft had taken all the fight out of her parents. They had lost heart, and finally they could do nothing to save themselves from the boredom and uselessness of old age. When they died, she missed them greatly but with the loss came a feeling of relief; they had found peace.

So Beth sat there in the saddle and listened to the small sounds of the night. Whatever Durant had done, nobody seemed to be worrying about it. If there had been big trouble, she knew that Carne and his crowd would have turned the town upside down to find Durant and administer their revenge. But nobody was out; it seemed as though she and Durant had the town to themselves. This thought warmed her until she realized how unfaithful she was being to the memory of a man. Lately she had begun to despise Paul for his weakness, but he'd been her man, accepted by her for better or worse.

Tears came to her eyes, but they were not tears for the loss of Paul Matheson. It was tension taking hold again. She wiped her eyes and vowed to get control of herself. But she needed the strength of Blake Durant, so, for a while at least, she'd let this big stranger dictate the course of her life.

* * *

Durant saw that the light was on, the stove afire and the back door open. He crossed the yard and flattened himself against the wall inches away from the door. Hearing no noise from inside, he drew his gun and walked in. Then his sweeping stare picked out the coffee stains on the floor and, further across the room the old blackened coffee pot lying on its side. Then he saw the man on the floor. A chill ran down his spine despite the warmth of the room.

He lifted Field in his arms and carried him across to the bunk. Lowering him carefully, he smoothed his gray hair back and made a quick examination. He discovered that Field had been shot in the back and the bullet had gone through the old, worn body, killing him instantly.

After that assessment of the facts, Blake made a quick search of the room but could find nothing to give the slightest clue as to the identity of the killer. He knew Field had put up a fight and he wasn't surprised. His brother was of the same stamp, born independent, and with the kind of grit that wouldn't let him take a backward step. Remembering the brother whom Blake had come to like immensely, Blake opened the pocket of Mort's shirt. He had seen Field put the letter from his brother in that pocket. Mort hadn't been able to read, so Blake doubted that he would have taken the letter out again. But he searched the room thoroughly, and finally he concluded that Mort's killer had taken the letter. Blake put up his gun and wiped his palm down his trail-dusty Levi's. Mrs. Matheson's troubles didn't seem as important now. In a way he blamed himself for Mort Field's death.

If he had minded his own business and let Field sell the Matheson woman a gun, perhaps the old man would be alive.

But he was dead and there was no changing that. Blake decided he could do nothing for the old man there and then that his fellow townsmen couldn't do better for him in the morning. Remembering his earlier decision to convince Beth Matheson to head for another town and seek assistance from a trustworthy lawman, Blake left the back room and went into the yard. He did not hesitate once his mind had been made up, returning immediately to where Beth Matheson awaited him.

He thought it best not to disturb her right away with the news of Mort Field's death, although he doubted if she'd known the old man well enough to be deeply affected by his death. Still, she had suffered enough for the time being, so after swinging onto Sundown, Blake merely said:

"Time to go."

Beth looked uneasily at him. "But where? Won't you tell me?"

"For the moment, just out of town. Do you know this territory well?"

"I've lived here for about seven years."

"Then pick a town that has a reliable lawman. We'll head that way."

With that Blake Durant gave Sundown his head. But before they left the laneway, three men appeared at its end. Blake drew rein and eased Beth against the fence. He hoped they hadn't been sighted, but a voice shouted:

"You there! Come out slow!"

Blake pulled Beth's horse about, hit it on the rump and said, "Head out—as fast as you can go!"

Beth's spirited horse took the bit between its teeth and lunged forward. By the time the horse reached the main street end of the lane way it was in full gallop. Beth heard shots behind her. Although she was loath to leave Durant behind to fight for her, she knew going back would do no good. She had difficulty turning the horse about in the main street, but once the animal caught the clean scent of the prairie, it again broke into a full gallop.

Back in the laneway, Durant had also turned Sundown, and the horse, responsive to his master's every move, despite the flurry of bullets coming their way, stood still under the lock of his knees.

Durant's gun blasted until he felt he had given Beth enough time to clear the town, then he put Sundown to a run. The big black pounded down the laneway and turned in a wide sweep into the main street. But before Blake could clear the end of the town, five men came charging out of the shadows to bar his way. He shot one down and heard him scream above the pounding of hoofs.

Then he was through the cordon of men and passing the jailhouse.

On the lighted boardwalk, gun bucking in his hand, was Horrie Sylvester. His tin star gleamed in the light hanging above his head—but Blake's gaze caught something else. He snapped a shot and Sylvester dived for the boards and rolled. Blake fired another two shots, then dropped his empty gun into his holster and rode hard.

He turned out of the town convinced that what he had seen clutched in Sylvester's left hand was Ambrose Field's letter to Mort. The letter taken from Mort Field by the man who had shot him in the back.

CHAPTER FOUR
No Country for Womenfolk

"Do you know a place where we can rest the horses?" Blake asked Beth Matheson as they drew their horses to a walk.

"There's cover just ahead, Mr. Durant. I remember coming this way once with my husband. It was a terribly hot day and we wanted to get into some shade. Paul discovered a small cutting in those foothills to our right."

Blake looked. The moonlight was weak, but there was enough of it to reveal the outline of an irregular sweep of crests, with many darker sections etched into them which he knew to be draws or the mouths of gorges.

He said, "It'll have to do. I don't want to go too far right now and I want to be sure you're safe."

The last part of his statement made Beth turn to face him. Back in town he had remained behind to see that she got free of danger. He'd exposed himself to gunfire and could easily have been cut down.

And his thoughts now, as they had been then, were only for her. What manner of man was he, and what did he want? Surely, she thought, no man, a complete stranger, would do so much, risk so much, for a woman ...

Durant had drawn a little ahead with Sundown picking out the trail, head bowed, walking slowly.

From time to time, Blake would warn her of a rock or a deadfall log, or a hollow. Some ten minutes later, she saw the small mouth of the familiar cutting with a flat rock on one side and a needle pointed boulder on the other, directly ahead.

"In there," she told him. "It's narrow but not far up it broadens out."

Blake nodded and then he concentrated on getting through the narrow gap without injuring the horses. When finally he came into a wider clearing, he took in deep breaths of the cool air. He could smell water and he told Beth there was a spring close by, one running underground which wouldn't show itself unless there were heavy rains. Beth was glad to hear him talk. It took her mind off the fact that she was alone with a man she scarcely knew. If he tried to make love to her, she wouldn't be able to stop him.

Durant left the saddle and climbed about the rocks. Minutes later he came back to her and stood mopping his brow.

"It'll do fine," he said. "Even in daylight this place can't be seen from the prairie, and the trail we came up was too hard for us to have left tracks. You could stay here for days, provided you had provisions, and you'd be perfectly safe."

For days? Beth felt a strange sensation run through her loins. Did he mean to keep her here? Now fear came.

Her husband was dead, so to some men she probably looked like an easy mark. Had Blake Durant, despite his air of nonchalance, had this in his mind from the very beginning? He had returned her money to her, but what was to stop him from taking it away again any time he wanted to? What could she do about it? She drew away from him and saw lines crease his broad, handsome brow. Her breath suddenly caught in her throat.

"There's something you should know," he said in a grave tone and Beth had to bite her lip to stop herself from gasping.

Was he going to try to win her confidence with some outlandish story of his past?

"Mort Field is dead," Blake told her, curious about the way she kept looking at him, as if afraid of something. Out here, in the seclusion of these rocks, he couldn't understand how an intelligent woman could fail to realize how absolutely safe she was. She should have been breathing deep sighs of relief and looking forward to an uninterrupted rest.

"Dead?" she whispered, shaking her head in disbelief. "But how? When?"

"When I left you to check him out, I found him lying on the floor in his place. He'd been shot in the back. Nothing in the place had been touched so there is no thought in my mind that it was robbery."

"But ..." Beth stopped and couldn't go on.

She remembered the kindly old man telling her to listen to Durant and to let him handle the business of her money and the killing of Tom Carne. She felt a deep sense of loss, as if Mort Field had been a dear old friend.

Blake said, "Later, when we were riding out of town, Sheriff Sylvester came charging out of the jailhouse and fired at me. He had a letter clutched in his hand, and I'm sure it was the same one I delivered to Mort Field from his brother down the Platte. That was why I was with Mort when you appeared, determined to buy a gun. I have no doubt in my mind that Sylvester killed Field."

Beth began to shake her head again, unable to believe this new tragedy had actually happened. "But why, Mr. Durant? Surely they didn't think an old man like Mr. Field could be a threat to them. He took me to the rooming house and ordered a meal for me. Then he said he was going back to do some work. He was that sort of man, kind and generous and they must have known it."

"I only know what happened and what I saw," Blake said. "You stay here and get some rest and I'll make my way back."

"You're going back?" Beth was stunned at the idea of it. She could see no possible reason for his returning to town.

"I have to go back," he said.

"Why?"

"To settle with Sylvester."

He said it in such a matter-of-fact tone that Beth was horrified. He seemed emotionless. "Some things have to be done," he said, then he drew his gun and began to ram shells into the cylinder.

"You mean to kill him?" she asked.

"It could come to that."

"But you scarcely knew Mr. Field. You just said that you'd only delivered a letter to him."

"His brother is a personal friend of mine, Mrs. Matheson, but he's not here to do what I know he would in like circumstances. I'll just have to do it for him."

"And what of the other idea, Mr. Durant? You spoke of seeking justice with another lawman. What about that?"

"It will have to wait. I might not be coming back this way and I don't like the thought of leaving scum like Sylvester untouched."

Beth watched him climb onto the big black. Suddenly she was terrified of being alone. "Couldn't I go with you?" she asked. "Perhaps I could help. I'm no stranger to guns, Mr. Durant."

Blake shook his head and said with finality, "This is man's work. Wait for me here. If I don't come back, go on alone and find somebody in authority to help you. That's the only way you'll ever avenge the murder of your husband."

With that Blake Durant pushed Sundown back into the narrow passageway. When he came out at the other end, be heard the close thunder of hoof beats. He drew rein and listened, reading from the sound that the riders had already gone past and were on the trail to Sonora in the south. How many there were Blake had no idea and he didn't much care. The only important consideration was that Sheriff Horrie Sylvester wasn't one of them. Although tied in with Carne, he couldn't desert his town and take up Carne's business without later having to answer for it to somebody. And he doubted if Carne, despite having established himself firmly in the town, would risk having his setup criticized openly.

So Blake went back towards town, riding easily. It took another hour to get there. Entering the main street, he saw that the lights of the jailhouse were still on. Blake left Sundown at the top of town in a dark laneway and went the rest of the way on foot.

He stopped outside the laneway wall of the jailhouse and listened intently. There was no noise at all from inside. Wanting to get this matter settled as quickly as possible, Blake began to edge his way to the back door. But before he reached the corner he heard a familiar voice growl:

"I hope to hell they bring him back alive."

There was a chuckle and then a voice Blake did not know said, "You itchin' to get your hands on the drifter, Ty?"

"Sure I am, Sylvester," said the other. "You figure I'm gonna carry this scar on my head for life and not want his hide? By hell, Carne shoulda let me go out too."

"Had to leave somebody to help me, Ty. No tellin' what this town might do in the morning."

Blake moved towards the back door. What riled him most was Sylvester's attitude. He'd killed an old man and it didn't bother him. Of all the breeds of men Blake Durant had dealt with, Sylvester's kind was the one he despised most.

He reached the door and put his ear against it. He had to know exactly where they were, sitting or moving, facing the door or looking the other way. In a business like this, a man seldom got more than one chance. So he had to get the first drop, take control and put on pressure as hard as he could. Knowing a little about Ty Pullen, he doubted if the gunman would break without a fight. The saloon incident had told him that.

He heard the scrape of a chair and then a yawn from one of them. When footsteps sounded, heading towards the front of the jailhouse, Durant moved up the steps. He took hold of the door knob and turned it very slowly. He heard a faint click as the tongue of the lock became free of its casing. Then he pushed the door in and followed it. Ty Pullen was almost to the front door, his hand out, reaching for the door knob.

Horrie Sylvester was seated at his desk, feet up on it, and Mort Field's letter was on the desk, between his legs.

Sylvester's mouth fell open and his face paled. He jerked his head back and his hat fell off. In the front of the office, Ty Pullen's jaw squared and his teeth parted to let a sharp hiss come out of his mouth. It was like the hiss of a snake.

Blake said, "Stay put, Pullen, and keep your hands empty. One false move, mister, and I'll forget this business has little to do with you."

Pullen worked his mouth soundlessly and his breathing became loud and rapid. "So help me, Durant."

Blake said, "Somebody will have to help you plenty if you push me."

Blake walked from the back doorway and crossed to Sylvester's desk. Sylvester gulped uncomfortably and sweat ran down his right cheek.

"Up slow, mister!"

Sylvester dropped his hands onto the edge of the desk and the muscles of his forearms became taut. But although Blake was aware that he was putting pressure on his hands, the lawman did not rise an inch out of his chair.

"Hurry it, damn you!"

Sylvester's body jerked and his feet scraped on the floor and he slowly started to rise. Muscles stood out on his scrawny neck and his breath wheezed out of his flabby mouth. To Blake Durant he looked as though he was certain he'd reached the end of the trail. Then Ty Pullen's right shoulder dropped and Blake turned just enough to cover him with his gun. Pullen's movement stopped.

For a moment Blake eyed him solidly. Then he said, "Unbuckle your gunbelt, mister, and let it drop."

Sylvester threw a desperate glance Pullen's way as he finally straightened to his full height. He kept his hands on the desk top, but Durant doubted if he would go for his gun. Sylvester didn't look the type to own that kind of hard grit.

Pullen shifted his hands to the buckle of his gunbelt. He unclipped the metal and held the belt loosely around his waist. "One day, Durant, one day real soon, I'm gonna shoot your interferin' guts out. I'm gonna—!"

"Drop it, mister!"

Pullen let the gunbelt fall to the floor. Without being told, he kicked it away, but Durant noticed that it was still within easy reach. He didn't care. He reached out and grabbed Mort Field's letter from the desk, giving Pullen the chance he needed if he was indeed the desperado Blake thought him to be. Pullen dived forward, pulled his gun free of leather as he hit the floor, and then he rolled.

Durant fired one shot which ripped Pullen's right wrist
open. Ty Pullen let out a howl of pain and the gun flew from
his fingers. He scrambled to his knees, holding his bloodied
wrist with his left hand, his face filled with hate and pain.

"You're a fool, Pullen," Blake told him, and then he pulled
Sylvester from behind the desk. He held the letter before the
sheriff's white face and said, "Mister, you took this from Mort
Field after you killed him."

Sylvester shook his head desperately and flecks of sweat
splattered over Durant's face. "No! You got it wrong, Durant!"

"Then how did you get the letter?"

Sylvester gulped, eyes wide with fear. "I ... I found it in the
street, Durant. Musta been somebody else took it. I heard
a shot and went to investigate and then I saw somebody
runnin' from Field's place. Likely a thief, I thought, so I went
after him, saw him drop that letter and I picked it up."

Blake Durant smiled thinly. "You're no better a liar than
you are a lawman, Sylvester." He tugged Sylvester's gun
from his holster and hurled it onto the desk top. The clatter
of the gun drowned the faint click of the front door lock
being released. But Blake Durant had seen Pullen's hand
go behind him. He didn't bother to stop the hellion, but
waited, watching Sylvester sweating until Pullen finally
made his desperate move. Durant saw the door open,
saw Pullen moving. He fired a shot which took Pullen in
the shoulder and helped him out the doorway with a rush.

Blake then walked after him, ignoring Sylvester. Pullen hit the boardwalk, smashed into the overhang post and then, in panic, dragged himself to his feet and lunged into the darkness. Blake Durant let him go because it was part of his plan.

He heard the scratch of boots on the hard floor of the jailhouse and turned quickly. Sylvester was leaning across the desk, clutching at his gun. He got it at his second try and then, his face filled with triumph, he straightened only to find Blake Durant's gun pointed at him.

Sylvester let out a howl of anguish and pumped off a shot without aiming. The slug whined past Blake's face, then stark terror entered Sylvester's face as Blake's Colt bucked twice. Both bullets hammered into the lawman and sent him reeling to the back wall. Sylvester bounced from the wall, the gun flying from his grip. Then he tottered forward until his legs buckled and he hit the floor on his knees in a praying attitude. He shook his head desperately for a moment before another wail came from him. Then he pitched forward and lay still, his face turned away from the empty eyes of Blake Durant.

Blake put Field's letter into his pocket and walked out of the jailhouse. He stopped on the boardwalk and let the cool night air wash over him. He doubted, in a town where so much roughriding had taken place, that few, if any, of the townspeople would bother to investigate the cause of the shooting. He doubted, too, that Ty Pullen, with two bullets having scarred him, would want more fight that night.

He had decided on these things when the sound of hoofbeats came from the prairie end of town. Looking that way Blake saw a black shape moving rapidly across the street. He turned and walked along the boardwalk to where he had left Sundown. The big black was pawing at the ground restlessly.

Blake quietened him, swung on, and rode from town.

CHAPTER FIVE

Closed Trail

Beth had not slept a wink since Durant had left her. She lay on her side, scratching at the ground with a small stick, remembering how sad her life had really been. She could hardly remember any phase of her life that had been wholly without pain or sorrow of some kind, even the early years when people had begun to call her beautiful and young men had eyed her unashamedly. She had taken a great interest in horses from an early age, and she'd discovered, when attempting to learn dress-making, that she was in fact a woman of the range and couldn't be anything else. So what was she going to do now, with Paul dead and their place burned down and Carne terrorizing her? Could she possibly hope for a solution to it all in the shape of Blake Durant, a stranger?

She was surprised, when she tried to remember what Paul looked like, that her recollection of him was vague. Had she really looked at him over the last year, or had she just accepted the fact that she was his wife and tried to make the best of it, blindly? This thought did more than surprise her; it pained her to think that she had accepted a situation which had brought only misery. Tears welled in her eyes, then rolled down her cheeks.

She needed sleep. The last three days had been hell, soul-destroying. She had lost faith in everything and everyone.

There was nobody to turn to until Blake Durant had come along, and although she was still somewhat suspicious of his motives, how could she be otherwise than in this vulnerable position? She was very much obliged to Durant for what he'd done. Beth sat up when she thought she heard a sound from the cutting. But after minutes had gone by and he didn't come, she lay back again. Loneliness pushed in on her and she began to cry again. There was just nothing at all to hang on to. The future looked completely forlorn and bleak.

She was still in this state of mind when Blake Durant rode onto the grassed clearing. Without speaking a word to her, he unsaddled Sundown and carried his gear to the far side of the clearing. Carefully selecting a place to sleep, he put the saddle down, spent some time shifting it about, then turned to her.

"It's done," he said, and she detected a note of weariness in his voice. Or was it regret?

"The sheriff's dead?" she asked, knowing the answer before Durant nodded.

"He's dead. I gave him as good a chance as he deserved."

With that Durant settled down with his head on the saddle and his hands behind his neck. In the gloom Beth couldn't tell if his eyes were open or closed. But she kept looking his way, wanting to speak, wanting to hear some words from him, no matter how insignificant. Then she was shocked to hear his steady, even breathing.

"Mr. Durant?" she whispered.

He gave her no answer and Beth called again, a little louder. This time Durant said wearily, "We might have a hard day of it tomorrow and we can't waste too much of tonight either. I'll wake you in four hours and we'll get an early start."

"Where have you planned to take me, Mr. Durant?" Beth asked.

Blake detected a tinge of worry in her voice, perhaps distrust. Why she felt this way he had no idea. He could move on and leave her here to do what she wanted all by herself. But he knew he wouldn't. He couldn't.

"I've thought about the territory hereabouts," he said. "What I know of it. My intention on passing through Sage Creek was to keep going down the Sonora Trail. There are bigger towns further on, and in one of them we'll find a lawman who can be trusted to look after your affairs for you. Not all law officers are like Sylvester."

"How far is it to Sonora?" she asked, wanting to keep him talking, reluctantly liking the drawl of his voice, feeling the assurance that was in the man himself coming through to bolster her own flagging confidence. He made it all sound so uncomplicated. You got on your horse and rode on, found a good law officer and everything would be dandy. He even made her forget, momentarily, about people like Tom Carne.

"I'm not sure how far it is," Blake said. "When you ask people for directions or distances in these parts, you get a dozen different answers. But most people say that Sonora is about a week's ride from Sage Creek."

"A week? A whole week?" Her voice rose. "But surely you don't expect me to travel that far in this hot weather."

"It's that or go back to Sage and wait, then I'll go on and send the right man or men back. Sleep on it and let me know when I wake you."

"I have no intention of sleeping," Beth said firmly.

Blake smiled to himself. He liked the woman, despite her switches in attitudes. She was beautiful and full of spirit. Given the chance she would make a good wife for the right man. He closed his eyes again and he fell into a deep sleep.

Beth lay there, looking at him, watching for any slight movement from him. She was determined not to sleep a wink that night, no matter how tired she was. And in the morning, when the raw sunlight was there to show things as they properly were, she would discuss the whole matter again, but on her terms. They would have to find somebody else to come with them, if they were to go all the way to Sonora. She would demand, and get, a chaperone. Smiling at the thought of how Blake Durant would feel about that, Beth closed her eyes. It was a great relief to feel the stinging strain going out of her eyes. Then she became drowsy, and her body relaxed.

The next thing she knew, a hand was shaking her by the shoulder and she looked up to find Blake Durant bending over her, a mug of coffee in his other hand.

* * *

Tom Carne cocked his head to one side and bellowed for his companions to be quiet. When he heard the drumming of hoofbeats more distinctly, he grinned. He drew his gun, shouldered two men out of his way, and hurried to where a cluster of boulders hid his view of the country below. Climbing one of the big rocks, he lay flat on his stomach and peered over. When he saw the solitary rider tearing along the edge of the narrow valley, he lifted the gun and took careful aim. The rider loomed up larger for a moment, then went from sight as he passed a clump of trees. Carne swore viciously, slid down and ran to the far edge of the rocks. When he again caught sight of the rider, he grinned evilly and again took aim. This time there was no obstacle to block his view of the man.

Carne's gun bucked and the rider lurched in the saddle and nearly fell. At the last moment, his hands grasped the horse's flying mane. The horse wheeled and the rider went sliding up its neck. Carne jumped to his feet and waved for his men to come running. They drew up abreast in time to see the rider somersault through the air and land on the broad of his back. A flurry of dust rose, hiding him from sight for a few seconds, then out of the dust cloud the man materialized, crawling on his knees.

"Fetch him up," Carne said and turned away, his face beaming. Three of his hands hurried down through the rocks to the wounded man who now lay on his stomach, his face in the dust. It was Ed Woodrow who reached him first. As he turned the man over, his face went white. Looking up, he saw that the others had also discovered the identity of the man.

"It's Ty," Woodrow breathed hoarsely. "Been shot before, too."

The other two, the runt, Cass Bailey, and a big man with a swollen right eyebrow, Dan Chandler, went down the slope to stand beside Woodrow.

"Hell, he's been hit three times and Tom only fired once," Bailey said.

Woodrow nodded. "Must have happened in town. Guess there's been trouble back there."

"Well, no sense in leaving him lying there," growled Dan Chandler. "Lift him up."

Together they carried the bulky body of the unconscious Ty Pullen back to Carne's hillside camp. When they lowered him to the ground and Carne came across, Woodrow said: "It's Ty, Tom. Wasn't Durant at all."

Carne's face tensed and his lips thinned. Then, looking at his men as if searching for their thoughts, he said, "What the hell was he ridin' a black for, and tryin' to get past? Serves him damned right."

Nobody argued against this. Carne spat on the ground, then swore under his breath and studied Pullen for a moment. "He dead?"

Chandler bent to put an ear against Pullen's chest. Unsure if he heard a heartbeat or not, he felt for a pulse and found a faint one.

"Ain't far off," was his opinion when he straightened up.

"Okay," said Carne. "Do what you can for him. Patch him up. We'll give him an hour while you boys rustle up some grub." With that, Carne walked away and sat brooding on his own, staring into the distance.

Woodrow, Chandler and Cass Bailey shifted Pullen into the shade and Chandler tore Pullen's shirt down. A slight puckering of his brow was all the expression he showed when he saw the bullet-shattered shoulder. Meantime Woodrow was inspecting the shattered wrist from which a splinter of bone showed through the gore. Bailey brought water and then Woodrow and Chandler washed the wounds. It was Chandler who broke away first, standing up and saying to nobody in particular:

"No damn use. A waste of time. Poison's set in. He won't make it."

"You sure, Dan?" came Carne's voice from the other side of the hillside clearing.

Chandler nodded. "He already had no chance when he came this way, Tom. You didn't have to waste a bullet."

"See if you can revive him," was Carne's cool answer. Chandler took the canteen from Bailey who was still washing the shoulder wound. He held it over Pullen's face and emptied it.

Woodrow jumped back from the splash of water, snarling, "Damn you, Chandler, ease off."

Chandler ignored him and Woodrow growled, "You wouldn't have the guts to do that, Chandler, if Ty was on his feet and unhurt. He gave you more'n you could take in town the other night, didn't he? You've had it in for him ever since."

Chandler's hard stare went to Woodrow, who took a step back, his mouth clamping shut.

Carne came back to them and said, "Enough of that. We got enough trouble finding Durant without fightin' with each other. Pullen was a good man and maybe I should have taken more care before I put a slug into him. But it don't matter, he'd have died anyway, we know that. Just get him awake. I want to know what the hell happened to him."

Chandler knelt beside Pullen and lifted his head from the muddied ground. He slapped Pullen's face lightly a couple of times and a groan came from the dying man. Bailey fetched another canteen of water which Carne took from him and poured over Pullen. A muscle in Pullen's cheek twitched.

Carne gave a grunt of satisfaction and forced water through Pullen's purpled lips. He then shook him roughly and blood flowed from the shoulder wound. Then Pullen's eyes opened and Carne grinned at him.

"Ty, you hear me? It's Tom. You hear me, mister?"

Pullen gulped for breath and looked vacantly at them. "Tom?" he croaked.

"Sure, Ty, me. Now you ain't hurt so bad you can't talk, Ty, and tell me what happened to you. Later we'll give you some strong coffee and you can take a sleep. But right now, Ty, you got to hold on and tell us a few things."

Ty Pullen took in a deep breath and then coughed up blood. The sight of it on his chest made him squirm in Chandler's grip. Deep fear showed in his sunken eyes.

"You're not hurt real bad," Carne lied. "So don't worry none. Now who the hell put those slugs into you?"

Pullen fought against Chandler's grip for a time but found he was too firmly held. He couldn't work his head about to see who held him.

"Damn you, Ty, tell me!" Carne yelled then and Pullen frowned as his stare went back to the head man. Again he gulped and again he coughed up blood. But this time he didn't seem to worry so much.

"Durant," he croaked.

Carne's eyes went wide with disbelief. "Who did you say, mister? Durant? You're loco!"

Pullen croaked again, "Durant, no mistake. Come into the jailhouse, accused Sylvester of killin' old Field. Tricked me into going for my gun and hit me when I did. Got me again when I made a run for it." Pullen paused for breath and the last vestige of color left his face. "Outside I heard more shots, then I got a horse up the street and rode out."

Carne held Pullen's jaw in his right hand and stared hard at him. "You're lyin'," he said. "We rode this way after Durant. We're close to him and we'll get him soon."

Pullen shook his head. "He's back in town."

Carne snarled an oath and suddenly hurled Pullen's head back to the ground. Pullen gasped and blood poured from his mouth. Then his head rolled to the side.

Carne came to his feet, still swearing. He crossed to the ring of rocks and stared back over the country they had travelled during the early part of the night. He couldn't believe that Pullen had spoken the truth. But why would he lie?

"No damn tracks," he said and, turning, eyed his men angrily. "Anybody see any damn tracks?"

Chandler said, "It was dark, Tom. We wouldn't have seen any tracks if they had been there."

"Then get down and check, damn you! Go right back a mile. See if we're makin' damn fools of ourselves chasin' a damn ghost!"

Three men immediately went for their horses. When they rode off, Carne shouted in his high-pitched voice, "Find them tracks! Find them!" He then crossed to where Woodrow was still kneeling beside Pullen. "He dead yet?" he snarled.

Woodrow nodded grimly.

"All right," Carne said. "You bein' his trail friend, mister, you bury him. The rest of you saddle up. We're pullin' out."

Carne went across to his horse and flung a saddle on it.

As he worked to prepare his horse for riding he grumbled to himself. When the saddle was on to his satisfaction, he pulled the horse roughly about and climbed up. He held the reins tightly between his fingers while he looked angrily down at Woodrow who was trying to prop a dead Ty Pullen up against a tree. Then Carne hit his horse into a run, shouting to the others, "Okay, let's go see!"

He went off the slope in a cloud of dust and was soon settling his horse down into an even run on the prairie.

All the outfit except Chandler and Woodrow followed him, with Chandler delaying long enough to give Woodrow a smile and say: "Do your chore, mister, then get lost. If I catch sight of you again, in Sage Creek or out of it, there'll be trouble."

Woodrow felt an agonizing cramp catch at his chest. All his life he had ridden with Ty Pullen. Through Ty's strength and ability, he had been able to find a niche for himself in several of the outfits that rode the owlhoot trail. But now, with Ty Pullen gone, he wondered if he could stand on his own. He had never tried.

Bending over Pullen's body he decided that he hated Dan Chandler. From the very beginning there had been bitterness between Chandler and Ty Pullen, which Woodrow had long since put down to a natural fight for the top gun position in Carne's outfit. In town two days ago, Chandler had tried to put the matter on the line and had been badly beaten up for his folly. But now Ty was dead, and that automatically made Dan Chandler the number one gun.

Was there a place left for him here? Would it be better to go his own way and link up with some other wild bunch? Settling down never entered his head. He hated hard work, hated sweating in the heat, hated the monotony of doing the same thing, day in and day out, for the meagre rewards farmers and cattle hands worked for.

Wiping sweat from his brow, Ed Woodrow looked about for shade. Finding some just off the clearing, he tested the ground and found it soft.

He scratched out a shallow grave with a dead tree branch
and dragged Ty Pullen's body into it. Then he went through
Pullen's pockets and took out his tobacco and bandanna,
a new one. Finally he exchanged his boots for Pullen's.
Then he realized that Pullen wasn't wearing his gunbelt. He
had always envied Pullen's expensive tooled gunbelt and
big gun. Although the gun would be too heavy for him, it
would have fetched a good price in the next town he passed
through. Woodrow went back to his horse and dropped the
tobacco in a saddlebag. He folded the new bandanna neatly
and put it on top, then he returned to kick dirt over his dead
friend's body. Finding that he hadn't made the grave deep
enough, he dragged some brush over it. Then, standing back
to survey his work, he figured he had done enough for Ty
Pullen, as much as could be expected, anyway. He walked
slowly to his horse, swung into the saddle and rode to the
edge of the ring of boulders. Far in the distance, a cloud of
dust told him where Carne and the others were heading. He
gauged that they were a good three miles away.

Woodrow had a few matters to attend to in Sage Creek
which could not be left undone. For one, had to get to Ty
Pullen's room at the saloon and go through his things.
Ty was not a flashy man, but he had a few articles which
Woodrow considered were his by inheritance.

That settled in his mind, he rode down the slope and
followed the dusty trail north.

* * *

Beth sat on a small boulder and sipped coffee gratefully. She couldn't remember having tasted anything as delicious in her life. The coffee was just as she liked it, strong and sweet without being sickly, as it was when Paul had made it for her. The smell of bacon frying added another pleasant touch. In the gray light of dawn, Durant knelt on one knee at the smokeless fire, acting as if he didn't have a care in the world. Remembering that at no time during the night had he come near her, Beth warmed to him and felt disposed to believe that her fears about his intentions were groundless.

Suddenly she felt let down, disappointed. It had been a long time since she had been tenderly treated by a man. Her husband had made his demands on her, naturally, but for a whole year she had spurned his advances, especially after she learned of his outlaw activities. That he could put his thieving, bloodied hands on her was impossible to think about, let alone allow to happen.

Minutes later, her coffee finished, Beth accepted the breakfast Durant brought to her. He handed her a fork and knife and then they ate. From time to time Beth was tempted to speak, only to stop herself because Blake Durant seemed too occupied with his own thoughts. When the meal was finished, she took his plate and eating utensils from him and crossed to get the canteen from the pommel of her saddle.

Durant said, "I'll do that."

"No," Beth refused with a smile, the first smile she remembered giving him. "This is woman's work."

As opposed to man's work, she reminded herself, which was killing and fighting. She emptied water on the soft ground, made mud and heaped it onto the plates and then into the battered old frying pan. That done, she rubbed the mud about until all the grease had been loosened, then she washed each of the utensils with clean water. When she had them shining she took them back to Durant looking pleased with herself.

"Good enough, Mr. Durant?"

"Fine," he said, and stacked them away.

Beth was a little disappointed by his lack of praise but then she decided that this was no time for a show of female annoyance. When she saw him climb into the saddle, looking completely refreshed after the few hours' sleep, she went back to her own horse, which was already saddled. Climbing up, she spent some time adjusting her skirt, and she flicked a glance at Durant to see if he was watching her. But Blake Durant had other things on his mind that early morning, including finding a way across these hills without being seen by Carne.

He rode into the cutting, turning only once to see if she was following. He was about to ride out the other end when he heard the thunder of hoofbeats from the prairie.

Swallowing a curse, he stopped Sundown and waited for Beth Matheson to get there, then he said, "They're coming back."

Beth didn't know what to make of this for a moment, but then she realized that if Carne passed them on his way back to town, the trail ahead would be free for them to travel.

"Won't that be all the better?" she said. "I mean, we can go on now and not have to worry about them."

"They'll reach town in an hour and discover what happened last night. That will put Carne after us with even more purpose."

Beth looked keenly at him. "But if we have a start on him, surely he'll never catch us. We'll have two hours."

"His kind travel fast," Blake Durant said, holding her look. He knew what was ahead, knew what it was like to be hunted. How would she stand up to the strain? There was no way of telling.

"But so can we travel fast, Mr. Durant. I'm not a stranger to hard riding and I've had to rough it many times. I can do so again."

Blake was silent. He wondered if it had been a stupid plan to take her along. But what else could he have done? To leave her behind in Sage Creek, would have been to leave her to the lustful violence of Carne.

"It will be harder perhaps than you think," he said.

"No harder for me than you, Mr. Durant. So please don't worry about me. I'll keep up and won't be the cause of any delay, you'll see."

The thunder of hoofbeats grew louder and then seven riders came into view. From the cover of the dark opening, Durant could see Carne and another big man out in front. Then came the runt he had watched so carefully in the saloon when he had confronted Pullen and Woodrow. The others were nondescript types he had often seen in cattle drives and in mining camps, men who followed the leader whoever the leader might be.

When they went past he gave them a few minutes and then he quietly moved Sundown into the open. The cloud of dust thrown up by the riders proved to be a perfect screen for them to hide behind. But before he put Sundown into a walk he said, "We'll take the first mile slowly and quietly. After that we'll let the horses run. With luck we should have plenty of distance between them and us by noon."

"I feel like riding right through till sundown," Beth said, still trying to get him to believe she wouldn't be a burden during the ride. Durant didn't reply but he set Sundown out for the side of the prairie. Beth Matheson followed, still wondering a great deal about him and worried that more of her personal feelings were changing towards him.

CHAPTER SIX
Wayward Gun

Ed Woodrow was so preoccupied with plans for his future that he hardly felt the warming sun on his face as he rode back towards Sage Creek. After burying Ty Pullen only an hour earlier, he had already forgotten about his former friend. To Ed Woodrow there was no sense in lamenting anything in life. He had followed that course of thought from the time his parents had been killed in a buckboard accident down in Texas when he was seventeen years old. Within a week of that double tragedy, he had sold up their small farm, auctioned off their personal belongings and trivial treasures, and hit the trail. He had never regretted doing it.

He turned around a huge outcrop of boulders, then some brush and stringy, near-dead trees—and he almost walked his horse straight into Blake Durant. Drawing rein, Woodrow halted, his face going pale and a quick rise of fear drying out his mouth so that he could not have spoken a word even on a gunpoint demand.

Then Durant said, "You're a long way out of your ground, Woodrow. How come?"

Woodrow's face was oily with sweat. Dan Chandler was one thing to worry about, but Durant was another. He didn't know what to say, didn't know what Durant might do.

So he stuttered without really saying anything, then his mind failed him completely.

"Shed your guns, mister, and turn your horse," Blake ordered. "You'd best ride with us for a bit."

Woodrow looked terrified at the suggestion. "Ride to where, Durant?"

"Wherever I have the whim to take you, mister."

"But, hell, Durant, I'm no use to you. I'd only be in the way. You got her money back and now you got her. What more do you want?"

Blake saw Beth's face tighten at the suggestion that she was Blake's woman. He said, "I want to keep you with us for a time, mister, so you can't go down that trail hollerin' that you passed us. Carne's gone back to town, and that suits us fine. Move now, take off your belt first, then ride ahead."

Woodrow watched Beth Matheson moving closer to him, peering into his face as if trying to recognize him. He worked his neck, feeling as if his shirt was choking him.

Then the young woman said, "You might have been one of the men who killed my nephew. I didn't think of it before, because it was so dark and so much was happening at the time to disturb me. But now I remember how you betrayed me, and betrayed your friendship with my husband. Perhaps I can identify you as one of them. That means you are a murderer, Mr. Woodrow, and a despicable one at that."

Woodrow shook his head in desperation. Then, seeing the woman's face go tighter and her eyes go cold he turned anxiously to Durant. "Hell, Durant, you know better than that. I ain't got the guts for killin'. I tag along, that's all, and I do the chores like unsaddling the horses. I get handouts while the others get a share of what's taken."

"When what's taken?" Blake asked.

"Banks, ranches, you know the score, Durant. Hell, you're no saint—you been around. The way you handle that gun, you been around plenty and likely you killed plenty."

Blake breathed in deeply, trying to hold his loathing for this coward in check. Then Beth Matheson stupidly worked her horse between Blake and Woodrow, and the latter, frightened to his boots, panicked. He kicked his horse forward, making it lunge past Beth. At the same time he drew his gun. Before Blake could stop him, he fired off a wild shot. The bullet whipped a long distance over Blake's head. Then Woodrow, thrashing the horse wildly, forced Sundown to swerve to avoid being knocked down. Blake Durant's gun roared and his bullet struck Woodrow between the shoulder-blades. The gun hand was plucked from the saddle as if by a giant's hand and hurled to the ground. Blake Durant came out of the saddle and went to the gun hand. He stood there, studying him expressionlessly for some time before he looked down the trail where Woodrow's horse with trailing rein was running wildly.

Then he left Woodrow, climbed back onto Sundown and moved up again to flank Beth Matheson. Her face was white and her hands were trembling.

"It couldn't be helped," he said. "I couldn't let him go on and give us away."

Beth could hardly look at him, she felt so disturbed. With all the talk of killing she had heard in her lifetime, she had never actually seen a man being killed. The suddenness and the cold brutality of it made her wince.

"Why ... why did you do it?" she asked, as if Durant's explanation fell far short of being satisfactory.

Blake did not bother to enlarge on his explanation but merely said, "We'd best push on. That shot will carry a long way on a dry morning like this in this kind of country. We might be lucky enough to get away with it, but I'd rather be on the safe side. So let's push on, fast."

Beth shook her head, not in argument against his suggestion but because she couldn't yet condone the killing. Her mind was terribly confused. On the one hand she understood what he meant, but on the other she could see him only as a killer, a cold, ruthless killer who seemed to have no feelings at all and certainly no regrets. Of course, Woodrow had been no good, but that didn't change things.

She said, "Are you going to leave him there?"

Blake shrugged. "His friends will find him later. Are you ready yet?"

Beth studied him impersonally, seeing him again for the stranger he was. And once more a terrible loneliness flooded through her. She felt she could very easily fall from the horse and just lie under the blast of the sun until she died. What was the use of going on? What was left in life for her?

Blake Durant, who had been watching her closely, surprised her by saying quietly, "Things will improve. When you reach rock bottom, you can only go up."

With that he moved his horse past hers, and after a solemn look again at Woodrow, he hit his big black into a run. This action, so abrupt and so decisive, caused Beth's horse to walk forward quickly and when Beth, hardly knowing she did it, released her hold slightly on the reins her horse burst forward eagerly and was soon in full gallop after Blake Durant and Sundown.

* * *

Dan Chandler wheeled his horse wide of Carne's and let the following riders tear past him. His action, seen by Carne, caused the mean-faced killer to swing the other way. When the others had passed him he sat his horse, choking on the dust thrown up at him. But as soon as he had cleared his lungs of the dust, he slapped his horse hard down the shoulder and converged on Chandler.

"What the hell you doin', Dan?" he asked. "You see something?"

"I heard a shot, Tom," Chandler told him, looking back along the chopped prairie trail.

"What damned shot? I didn't hear nothin'."

"I heard it," Dan Chandler insisted. "A long way off, a rolling echo, near wind-thinned to nothing. But I heard it."

"You're loco."

The others, having gone on only a little way, had now returned and were bunching.

Carne asked, "Any of you hear anything? A shot maybe?"

"Thought I did," said Cass Bailey and another man nodded, backing him up. "Couldn't be right sure," the man put in.

Carne's mouth twisted. "Damned if I did," he muttered as if challenging somebody to try to convince him. He then studied Dan Chandler grimly, knowing his top hand as a man who made few mistakes. Chandler had never shown ability in forming a plan for operations of any kind, but once a plan was outlined to him, he could be relied upon to carry it through to the end, no matter who or what got in the way.

"Who'd be out there firing off shots?" Carne asked.

"Woodrow's back there," Chandler reminded him.

"Woodrow couldn't shoot his toe off with a cannon," Carne snarled. "And Durant's back in town."

"Maybe not," Chandler said.

Carne's mouth gaped. "Maybe not?" he repeated. "How come, Dan? Hell, quit talkin' in riddles and say what you got in that fool mind of yours."

Chandler worked about in the saddle and felt the eyes of all the other men fixed on him. He liked the feeling of being the center of attention. He had worked hard enough to get into this spot and he wasn't about to let go of it lightly.

So he said, speaking very slowly, "Well, Tom, we know Durant left town and we know he went back. Also, we know he has the Matheson woman with him."

"How do we know that?" Carne barked.

"It stands to reason, don't it?" Chandler went on, untroubled by Carne's hard tone. "Durant tackled Woodrow and Pullen about the money Beth Matheson gave them. When he got the money he must have gone back to her. She's a fine looking woman, and Durant's the kind that would win her easy. My guess is Durant brought her out of town where she'd be safe and—"

"They rode out together last night, early," put in Cass Bailey. "There was two of them in that lane way and one lit out first. Durant stayed back awhile, delaying things, and I reckon it'd be a woman he'd be protecting."

Carne drew in a ragged breath. "Don't nobody in this outfit tell me nothin'?" he shouted, his eyes blazing.

"Thought you knew," Bailey said in a guarded tone.

Carne snarled at him, then quickly regained his composure. "Okay," he said to Chandler again. "So Durant left town with the woman and didn't go back with her. Meantime, he killed Sylvester. So now you want me to believe that Durant ..."

Carne stopped and threw a vicious look at Dan Chandler. He began to nod his head and mumble to himself, then Chandler finished with:

"So he linked up with the Matheson woman, and they hid out. When we didn't find no tracks up further, we doubled back. And somewhere along the way, Durant and his woman saw us, bided their time and then pushed on. That's how they ran into Woodrow."

Carne pulled a hand across his face and picked up his reins. The hard ride to that point had not wearied him in the least. But it had brought so much sweat out of his body that his shirt clung to his back.

"Yeah," he admitted. "It could be."

"It's got to be," Chandler said, milking the last bit of importance from the incident. When Carne wheeled his horse and began to ride on, he allowed himself a thin smile of satisfaction. From this point, Dan Chandler, he told himself, you ain't got nothing to worry about. Could be that, one day, when somebody cuts down Tom Carne, which is sure enough coming, you'll inherit yourself a well-trained outlaw mob. He broke into a chuckle and got his horse going. Although he trailed the rest of them and ate their dust, nothing could take the happiness out of his black soul.

* * *

It was mid-morning before Durant decided to reduce speed. He felt as if he could go on forever, because the day was not as hot as each day of the previous week had been. A fresh wind that blew into their faces had the slight smell of rain in it. But as yet there was no evidence of rain clouds to make progress difficult.

After the sweating horses had settled down into the slower pace, Blake sensed that something was troubling the young woman, and his mind went back to what Ed Woodrow had said about his laying a claim to her. Looking at her now, he said, "No worries?"

Beth's brow puckered. "Only the heat. And I'd like a bath."

"We should pass a creek late today or tomorrow. There's no desert country down this way."

"Thank goodness for that. How do you think we've progressed, Mr. Durant?"

"As well as anybody who might have taken it into their minds to follow us, Mrs. Matheson. If we had two hours' start at the beginning, that's what we still have."

"That's a mercy," she said, fidgeting with a button on her blouse while her gaze swept the country about them. It was good cattle country yet there was no evidence of stock on it. She noticed then that Blake Durant was also taking in the country with his keen eyes.

"You like being on the trails, don't you?" Beth said.

Durant shrugged, but she noticed that his eyes had changed. A kind of warmth had come into them. He said, "Some men were meant to dig and turn soil, some were meant to rig fences and drive and brand cattle, and some were meant to live in towns. Me, I guess, lately anyway, I was just meant to go on."

"On to where?" she asked, liking the different tone of his voice.

Durant smiled faintly. "Who knows? Maybe there's an end to the trail somewhere."

"Then you're looking for something," she said. "But you don't know what it is. Don't you think it's all so useless when you do that?"

Blake smiled thinly at her. "Only, Mrs. Matheson, when you've never known it before," he said and he saw her tighten her mouth as she often did when something confused her.

"Before?" she asked, puzzled. He merely nodded and rode on, and she felt again that he had pushed her aside, disregarded her as if she was of little consequence. This hurt her more than a little, and the fact that it did annoyed her. She was coming to like and trust this man, yet the barrier between them remained. Why she wanted that barrier to be broken down, she had no idea. Their association was that of a woman in trouble and a man with a gun. No more. And she promised herself right then that this was how it would be in the end.

They rode on, slowly now, into the waves of heat. But the breeze remained, giving them some relief from the hot sun. Durant kept an eye on the horses and noticed that Sundown had shown no inclination to shorten stride. Beth Matheson's horse seemed to be bearing up well, too, although from time to time its head drooped.

As for the woman, despite her determination to match Blake in everything, he could see dark shadows under her eyes and the strain in her face was deepening. He figured she might see out today all right and after a night's rest would come up well and keen again in the morning. But he felt she would begin to tire in a few days and would then begin to slow him up.

So what? he told himself. He was committed to get her to Sonora, and he'd do that if he had to carry her.

Noon came and Blake could feel the sun burning his skin. On his own, he would have just pulled his hat down more firmly and pushed on. But with her along, he decided to make this trek in stages. If Carne and his hellions caught up, too bad.

With that in mind he worked gradually in towards the hills. He let a dozen of them go by until he found a wide passageway leading between two of them. Beyond the opening of the passageway, he saw that the ground was hard.

So he said, "Wait here, don't move another step."

Beth eyed him curiously. "Where are you going?"

"To make a false trail."

He rode into the passageway, letting Sundown shift about as he liked. When he came back he told Beth to climb down out of the saddle, and doing the same himself, he led his horse along the very edge of the hard ground. Beth followed him, wondering if the sun had got to him, but she was too hot and tired to argue. When he finally stopped a hundred yards from where the mouth of another gorge began, she felt she couldn't walk another step.

Blake said, "We'll take an hour's rest here, Mrs. Matheson. I think the horses can use it. Freshened up, they'll be able to outstrip Carne's outfit if they've gained ground on us."

Beth found she didn't even care about Tom Carne and his killer friends. At the same time she was aware that Durant had spared her by pretending it was the horses he was worried about. She found shade against a shoulder of rock and sat down, pushing her head back and breathing in deeply. Half a day had gone by but there were still six and a half to go, and six nights to spend with this stranger. She put the troublesome thought from her mind and closed her eyes.

Slowly, the saddle cramp went out of her body, and her skin, which she felt was drying to parchment, began to cool. She had no intention of sleeping, but gradually her breathing became more rhythmic and she found herself dozing off. She fought off sleep for a time but then succumbed to it, telling herself it didn't matter, that nothing mattered.

Finally Durant's hand on her shoulder brought her awake. She looked up into his face and smiled.

"Time to make another move, Mrs. Matheson," he said.

"All right," she said, matter-of-factly, then took his outstretched hand and let him pull her to her feet. She stood close to him then, still holding his hand. She could feel all the strength of the man in that grip. A thrill ran through her body and she quickly withdrew her hand and stepped back.

Durant turned away and mounted his horse. He rode off and she had to hurry to get into the saddle and follow him.

For the rest of the afternoon, Durant set a steady pace towards the empty prairie. As the day cooled, Beth began to think of her life as it had been and decided there had been little joy or happiness in it, in fact, she had been a fool to put up with it. In the future, if she had a future, she would hire some good men and boss her own place. The responsibility in this attracted her, and she knew she was as good at ranch chores as her husband had ever been. In fact, during the last year, most of the hard part of running the ranch had fallen to her. Paul was mostly away and she had been alone, but strangely she hadn't been lonely. It was only when Paul returned that she had felt loneliness.

Finally they reached prairie country. Durant stopped Sundown a few yards ahead of her and looked into the western sky. She followed the direction of his gaze and marveled at the color there. It seemed as if every color under the sun had been splashed across the horizon.

"It's beautiful," she said. "I've rarely seen anything like it."

"Up north there are a lot of sundowns like this," Durant said. "I remember a valley six or seven miles wide and all of fifty miles long. On each side high mountain ridges shut it in, and here and there deep gorges and ravines cut back into the ridges and there are green meadows and tumbling waterfalls. All the hills are timbered to their crests. It's even more beautiful than this."

Beth stared at him, astounded. She had never heard him talk like this. Usually his speech was blunt, and he said only enough to get his point across.

"You make it sound like a place you shouldn't have left," she said. "Why did you?"

"Things happen," he said in his blunt way and she realized the moment of knowing him better had ended. Then he added, "My horse can smell water. Perhaps it's the creek you wanted."

And with that he went on, walking the horse, in no hurry. Behind them stretched the prairie, empty, noiseless. Beth felt a deep satisfaction creep over her. The day was finished. Now there was the night, perhaps a bath, then some food and a long, long sleep. She smiled, taking in a deep breath of the fresh sundown air and followed him without complaint or question. They rode for another hour before they found the creek. It was shallow and not very wide, but the water was cool and it ran slowly. After she had bathed, Beth walked back to the camp Durant had already made. He had their meal ready and was already sitting down enjoying his when she walked up. Looking at him now, she couldn't keep herself from smiling warmly.

"That was worth all the riding and worrying and being hunted, Mr. Durant. Don't you want to clean up?"

"I already have," he told her and Beth was surprised to notice that his dark skin did have a clean gloss to it and that his hair was wet.

She wondered where he had bathed, and blushed at the thought that it might have been close to her. She had been enjoying herself so much in the creek that she had splashed about like a child. Perhaps he might have—

She felt her cheeks go hot, and Durant, looking straight at her, said, "The creek turns sharply a quarter mile up. We'll go that way tomorrow and head into the hills. I've been thinking that Carne will suspect we've headed for Sonora and will know the reason why. So he'll bide his time and not exhaust himself. It may not be until tomorrow or the next day that he catches up with us."

"You think he will?" she asked him nervously as she took her meal and settled down to eat.

"It's got to happen."

"But why? Surely we've made good time today."

"He'll have made better. When we eat we'll push on, and use a little of the night. When we find a tight corner, we'll rest."

And with that Blake Durant continued with his meal. Later, after they had travelled five more miles and Durant had found a suitable place for their night camp, Beth lay in her blankets and thought a great deal about him. How tall he was. And how strange. One moment he was like a boy, taking from his surroundings all the happiness he needed.

She wondered what kind of woman he would be attracted to, and decided it would probably be the gay, frivolous kind, with ribbons and bows. Men were so stupid that way; they thought a woman had to be decked out in frills to be feminine. She was almost asleep when she heard him mount up and ride away and she was about to shout to him, wanting to know what he was up to. But then he was gone, lost in the night. She sat up, then she settled back, realizing he would have spoken to her if it had been important.

So, trusting him as she had never trusted a person in life, Beth Matheson fell asleep.

CHAPTER SEVEN
Blood Creek

Blake Durant rode back down to the creek where they had eaten their evening meal and then he turned Sundown's head south. The big black's hoofs left clear tracks along the creek bank. He rode for half an hour before he sent Sundown into the creek and walked him back. He passed the earlier campsite and walked Sundown up the creek for another quarter of an hour before he returned to where Beth Matheson was sleeping.

Making no noise, he unsaddled the big black and dropped to the ground, using his saddle for a pillow and the sky for a blanket. It took him no more than a few minutes to go into a sound sleep.

* * *

Tom Carne was in a sour mood when he reached the body of Ed Woodrow on the prairie trail. Chandler was right. Durant was in front of him, which meant he and his men had travelled dozens of wasted miles.

Leaving Woodrow for the buzzards, he pressed on and all through the long, hot day, he kept his men on the move, stopping at noon and again in mid-afternoon, to rest the horses and have a meal. The beauty of the country didn't impress him at all. He felt only the heat and the drive of the wind. Nobody spoke to him all day, not even during the two meal breaks.

By sundown he was tired but in no way ready to give up. When he reached the creek where Durant and Beth Matheson had stopped, he had not yet made up his mind whether to press on through the night or to let the men and horses rest. He had already sensed the spirit of rebellion in some of them, Dan Chandler included, but Tom Carne was not a man to worry about such trifles. Those who wanted to go on, could. And those who wanted to stay behind could do so—with bullets in them.

Dan Chandler was beside Carne as their horses watered in the creek. Chandler had been watching Carne carefully all afternoon and he knew that the determination to get Durant would drive Carne to the point of exhaustion, even if it meant killing the rest of them.

So he said, "Durant's a tricky customer, Tom."

Carne's head jerked about and his cold eyes settled on Chandler.

"So?" he growled.

"He knows he's being hunted and if he's found he'll be killed. He won't take any chances."

Carne sneered across at his top hand. "Say it, plainer, damn you!"

Chandler removed his hat and raked a hand through his hair. He looked less tired than any of the others who were now lined along the bank watering their horses.

"He'll likely lay false trails."

Carne looked puzzled. "He's headin' for Sonora, ain't he? So how come he'd waste time leaving false trails?"

"In his position, I would," Chandler said. "Especially with a woman to take care of. He'll play for time."

Carne thought grimly about this and shook his head. "No, I'm not buying that, Dan. Durant has a good start, or did have. He'll go on just as fast as he can go. All the way he'll be thinking of me dogging his trail and he'll push himself and the girl to the limit. We ain't stoppin', Chandler, not for anything."

"What if we take the wrong trail ourselves, and lose him?"

"We won't, damn you!"

"The men need an hour or two anyway," Chandler said stubbornly. "If you keep pushing them, Tom, by tomorrow night they'll be ready to fall."

"Then let 'em fall."

Dan Chandler pulled his horse away from the creek and rode along the line of men.

Carne eyed him suspiciously, watching to see if he spoke to any of them. He could feel something growing against him and if trouble came Chandler was the likely one to start it.

He saw Chandler go to the end of the line and look south across the creek, towards Sonora. Carne had been there many times, and the last time he'd been forced to leave in a hurry. But he didn't mind going back, not with the men he had along with him this time. Sonora was a big, prosperous town. After they took care of Durant, he could see no harm in taking Sonora apart. The bank would be bulging at the seams with the money deposited from the year's cattle sales.

Tom Carne brought his hand away from his gun and rubbed it across the stubble of his jaw. He hated this trail burning. A quick ride then some fierce action suited him fine. Riding on and on only made him more vicious. He dragged his horse roughly out of the water and looked bleakly about him. Chandler was smart, or seemed to be. He had been right about Durant being in front of them. Woodrow's body proved that. And Chandler could also be right about Durant leaving false trails. When he was being hunted himself, it was a ploy he always used. Strike one trail, double back, strike another, double back and strike a third. Then get to hell out of there.

He looked into the sky and knew that within ten minutes it would be dark. He meant to press on for a few more hours which would get them perhaps another ten miles closer to Sonora. But what if it was the wrong trail? They'd have to come back and start again.

"Dan," he called finally.

Chandler came up the creek towards him.

The men had drawn back, their canteens filled, their horses watered. They stood grouped like men waiting for a saloon to open, their faces drawn and haggard, weariness etched deeply into every one of them.

Carne said, "I been thinking. Maybe we should take an hour or so layup. Get some grub cooking and plenty of coffee. You look after mine, will you?"

Chandler nodded grimly. Ty Pullen had always sat with Carne and discussed matters while the others did what chores needed doing. But he was being relegated to fetch Carne's supper. The thought riled him, knowing as he did that every man in this rough bunch wouldn't fail to realize Carne's motives.

But, not yet ready to protest, Dan Chandler went off. Carne rode his horse up the small clearing and stopped dead when he saw the marks on the ground where two people had been. There were a few cold beans left on a rock. Carne came out of the saddle and angrily called Chandler over.

"He's in a damned hurry, is he? Well, what about them beans? You reckon he's so damned scared of me that he sits down and has himself a real comfortable meal? Maybe he used a napkin, too, 'cause he had a woman with him."

Chandler swung off his horse and inspected the beans, wondering if Durant was getting careless or extra smart. But he kept his conjecture to himself, seeing Carne's mood become increasingly ugly.

When his top hand made no comment, Carne growled, "So the layup is already finished. Tell the men we're moving out."

Chandler jerked about, his face tightening. "They won't like it, Tom. They're beat. If you push them through the night, they'll be an ugly bunch in the morning."

Carne dropped his right hand onto his gun butt. "You gonna tell them or not, mister?"

Chandler's mouth tightened a little before his shoulders sagged. "Sure, Tom, sure. Don't get heated up."

"Then don't argue with me, big man. Never. Don't you ever do that!"

Dan Chandler walked off leading his horse. It took him several minutes to round up the men again and tell them they were moving on. Nobody protested but Chandler saw several throw hard looks Carne's way. Then Carne was with them and pushing across the creek. He rode into the settling night, about twenty yards ahead of Chandler, with the rest strung out behind.

* * *

Beth awoke to find Durant hunched over a small fire warming beans while a coffee pot steamed at his elbow. She had seldom had a more rewarding sleep in her whole life.

Every part of her thrilled to the freshness of the morning and she stretched out luxuriously, feeling vigor surge back into her body. Throwing off her blanket, she remembered with a jolt where they were and what trouble she was in.

So she asked, "Do you think its sensible making a fire, Mr. Durant?"

Blake had heard her stir and then rise, but now looked at her for the first time. He was amazed to see the brightness of her eyes and the glow of color in her face.

"It won't matter today," he told her. "Wash and then come and eat. We'll move out in ten minutes."

He walked away then, leaving her beans in the pan. Beth washed in the creek and came back brushing her long hair. She ate her meal in silence but when Durant brought her horse across, she felt compelled to ask:

"Where did you go last night, Mr. Durant?"

"To lay a false trail."

"What's that?"

"I left tracks leading the other way. It won't delay them long, that's if they follow it. But every minute we gain is a help."

With that he swung onto Sundown and led the way off the little clearing.

For three hours he rode ahead of Beth, not speaking a word, and she began to wonder if she had in some way offended him. Or perhaps he was sick of nursing her along the trail and wanted to be on his way. As they broke into open country, she drew level with him.

Looking straight at him she asked, "What's wrong?"

"Wrong?"

"You've been quiet all morning. Have I done something to upset you?"

"No," he said shortly.

"Then what is it?"

"Maybe it's the opposite, Mrs. Matheson," Blake said then, turning to look at her. Beth felt blood rush to her cheeks.

"The opposite of what?" she forced herself to ask.

"The opposite of upsetting me, ma'am. You're an attractive woman and this is very beautiful country. You belong to it and I think I do. That's what I've been thinking about, about you and this country."

"Oh." Beth could think of nothing else to say.

"I don't want to see you killed, and I feel there's a good chance of that happening if we continue on as we're going. It might be better to lay this trail and then double back."

"Go back to Sage Creek, you mean?"

"Yes."

Beth was thoughtful for a time. They were still in the open and the sun was hot on her face. "But there's nothing for me back there, Mr. Durant."

"No?" He was looking straight at her again in that unsettling way he had. She felt excitement catch hold of her.

"Nothing at all," she managed to reply and then he smiled—shyly, she thought, and went on.

They rode for another three hours before Durant struck their noon camp. They ate a quick meal of jerky and biscuits, washed down with strong, black coffee. When Durant brought her horse to her this time, she remained close to him, staring straight into his solemn, but handsome face. Her lips were moist and her bosom heaved under the stress of an upsurge of emotion. Durant put a hand gently on the nape of her neck and drew her to him and Beth found herself responding. When he kissed her, she closed her eyes and lay against him, fearing that she would burst with happiness.

Then he broke away, smiled again, and helped her onto her horse. From the saddle, Beth asked, "Why did you do that?"

"I couldn't help it. It's the day and you; the combination was too much for me."

"It was nice," she said. "And I didn't mind. I didn't mind at all."

"I'm glad," he said, and then he rode off, leading her into the foothills.

* * *

Dan Chandler stopped and Tom Carne, reining up, glared at him. The others were far behind, silent and tense.

"What now?" Carne growled.

"We've gone far enough the wrong way, Tom," Chandler said. "You know we have, but you won't admit it."

Carne frowned darkly. "I'm wrong and you're right, mister, is that how you see it?"

"That's how I see it, Tom. I'd be no use to you if I didn't try to change your mind. Durant's tricked us. He left a trail back there that led us straight to the creek. It was natural to figure he headed straight across the creek towards Sonora. But maybe he isn't going to Sonora."

"Where the hell else could he go?"

Chandler shook his head. "Not right away, anyhow. Durant feels he has time on his hands and he knows he can't outrun us. So he means to out-think us. I think we should go back. The time lost means nothing because he won't be pressing on fast with the girl to worry about."

Carne swore under his breath, then he turned as the others came up. He gave Chandler a warning look before he announced, "We're going back to the creek. We'll rest there. We've wasted half a night but that don't matter. We'll rest up again for a couple of hours like we did back aways, and then we'll spread out and pick up the right trail. Next time our friend Durant isn't gonna fool us."

Carne's admission seemed to make the men feel a lot better and he knew then that every one of them had been of the same mind as Chandler but hadn't had the guts to come forward and protest. Leading off, he put his horse into a run and galloped all the way back to the creek. There he unsaddled his horse and while the men searched about for comfortable places, he walked along the creek bank to the south until he saw where Durant had entered the creek. Grinning to himself, he checked out the other bank. Finding no tracks, he walked the shallows back to the camp and past it. When he returned an hour later, he nudged Chandler awake and said:

"Okay, we're moving out. He headed for the hills." Chandler, who hadn't been sleeping at all, rose without complaint. He quickly aroused the other men, and when Carne led off again up the creek, he followed. Carne made sure each of them saw the tracks clearly leading out of the creek before he charged his horse up the bank and headed for the hill trail.

For half the morning he kept pushing on, shaking off the terrible weariness that was beginning to ache through his body.

His eyes stung and his mouth was constantly dry despite the many sips he took from the canteen during the hot ride. He followed a clear trail along a valley wedged between towering hills, but the wild beauty of it failed to impress him. He hardly saw it as his mind seethed with thoughts of Durant's bravado. The drifter had not only brazened it out with Pullen, Woodrow and ten of his hired hands, he had killed Sylvester, had almost killed Pullen, and later he'd put paid to Woodrow.

Of those, Sheriff Sylvester was the only one Carne thought would be hard to replace. He had worked Sylvester into a position where he could make him lick his boots if they got dirty. And he had, by achieving that, got his hands firmly on Sage Creek and all its citizens.

But Durant had put a hole in that sack and most of Carne's ambitions had fallen out. Most, but not all. When he caught up with Durant and killed him, everything would be ready to trim back to normal again. He might even make Chandler the new sheriff. That would leave him out on a limb and in no position to bolster his position with the men. He'd be right where Carne wanted him.

Smiling now, Carne stopped his horse when he saw the tracks of two horses leading directly towards the hills.

He wondered if this was another trick on Durant's part, to gain him time to go into hiding and rest up again.

To make sure, he sent Chandler and three others along the edge of the bench as he waited in the shade, resting eyes which were stinging from the sun glare. Chandler returned fifteen minutes later and shook his head.

"Nothing up there, Tom."

"You sure? You checked it out?"

"If there were any tracks we'd have found them," Chandler said sourly, the extra duty having made him realize that Carne was going to ride him into the ground.

"Well, I guess I'll have to take your word for it, Dan," Carne said, grinning crookedly at him. "We'll push on, right?"

Carne turned and eyed each of the men in turn before wiping sweat from his brow and adding, "Won't be long, now. Soon as we get Durant and kill him off, I'm gonna let you boys have some time in town. We'll get ourselves some women and tear that saloon apart."

Carne didn't worry about the lack of response to this offer, but he led off again, watching the trail carefully. He rode for another twenty minutes before he found a place where the two he was hunting had rested. Coming out of the saddle, Carne spent a considerable amount of time checking the ground and brush that sprouted out of the rocks. Satisfied, he called for Chandler to make camp, and on his own he walked up the narrow trail, following the clear tracks of two horses.

CHAPTER EIGHT

Sighted!

It was close to sundown on the second day out of Sage Creek that Blake Durant began to get tense again. All during the afternoon Beth had watched his nervousness grow. Every mile or so he stopped and checked the trail behind them, as if expecting at any moment that Carne and his hellions would burst into view. She felt no great fear herself, mainly because Blake Durant was there, and in some inexplicable way she trusted him without reservation. When those killers came, she was positive he would know what to do.

Riding up beside him as the trail broadened out a little, she said, "Do you think they'll come soon, Mr. Durant?"

He nodded. "We've got to make a camp and rest the horses. If we don't we'll be finished by morning."

"Whatever you say," she told him. Since the moment he had kissed her, she had retained the feel of him against her body. His body was so firm, so strongly built. She had felt like a soft fabric in his embrace. It was a wonderful feeling, one she knew she would remember for the rest of her life, even if it didn't go any further. She doubted if it would because since that moment of contact, Durant had withdrawn into himself. His only talk during the day had been about the trail, about the time it was taking, about the distance which still had to be travelled. Five more days lay ahead of them and she knew he was afraid they wouldn't make it.

Suddenly Durant drew ahead and came out of the saddle. He dropped the reins, as he always did, and Sundown stood still. She had come to admire the attachment between horse and man. The big black answered his every command, sometimes even anticipating what the order would be. It was a strong yet gentle relationship which she knew had been born of long understanding. But how long? For how many years had this strange man been drifting along the trails?

Beth realized she knew nothing at all about him. He had never mentioned his past or his connections with people. Certainly he must have had his share of women. It was not reasonable to expect that a man like he would be left alone by the loose women in the towns he'd passed through. Thinking this, Beth felt a twinge of jealousy.

Then Durant brought her out of herself by saying, "This will do fine. There's cover on three sides and the open side is fed by a steep slope. To get to us, they'll have to come in single file, and slowly."

Beth looked at the small rock-cluttered clearing and decided he was right. It was so small that the pair of them and the horses could barely fit into it. Which meant that tonight she would be very close to him, disturbingly close. But since Blake Durant was making all the decisions, she walked her horse past him and let the animal find a place for itself. She sank down on a small rock ledge and let her hair fall free, swinging it about her shoulders until she felt the air sweeping through it. She was hot and dirty and she longed to be in that little creek again.

Durant had unsaddled Sundown and her horse and stacked the saddles in the middle of the opening they had walked through. Now he was packing rocks on each side of them, making them secure. Fear lifted inside her when she realized that he had not bothered about defense the previous night, but now he was making careful plans against an attack. Did that mean he expected an attack tonight?

She rose and asked, "Wouldn't it be better to go on if you think they're that close? I can ride right through the night if needs be."

He shook his head. "We've come far enough."

"But why not, Mr. Durant?" she said, kneeling beside him. "You can't expect to win out against all of them. There might be a dozen of them."

He shook his head. "Eight."

Beth gaped at him. "But how did you know that?"

"I saw them, Mrs. Matheson. They're only an hour behind us and coming up fast. They've scented the kill and nothing will slow them now."

"Then why can't you lay a false trail again? If it worked once, it will surely work again."

"We're in the wrong kind of country, ma'am," he told her stubbornly.

"There's only one way over the top of this ridge and that's the way we came. They'll know that, too. So, for the moment, sit down and be quiet. I've got to prepare for it."

Beth was shocked by his sudden rudeness. But she moved away from him. She sat down and watched him pile rocks about the saddles. Then he lay down and took out his gun. He rose, dusted himself down and seemed satisfied.

He said, "They'll come tonight or at first light. I want you to lie flat and don't move. I have every chance of fighting them off and wounding a couple of them. If I can do that, I'll be able to slow them up for another day at least. That will give us the chance to push on across the hill and down onto the other plain. We might find people there."

Beth didn't know what to say. She could visualize the trouble ahead with this one man fighting eight desperate hellions. He would have no chance at all. And once they had put paid to him, what would stop them coming up and killing her, or worse? She shuddered at the thought of their hands on her body, tearing at her. More than once she had seen Ty Pullen ogling her as if he wanted to rape her. She had mentioned this to her husband at the time, but he had laughed at the suggestion. Pullen was, he had told her, more interested in drink than in women. But Beth knew she had been right.

"Did you manage to recognize any of them, Mr. Durant?" she asked.

He shook his head. "No. But one of them was riding far out in front, looking as if he couldn't wait to reach us. I expect that was Carne."

"Do you know him at all?"

"Never laid eyes on him that I know of, Mrs. Matheson. But I guess he runs to the usual pattern."

"He's an ugly little man with a mean mouth and small black eyes. One look at him and you realize that all he has in his mind is killing. His men and the whole town are afraid of him. When he killed Paul, he stood there gloating over it. I wanted to go and tear at him with my bare hands, and I might have if my nephew hadn't got in the way."

Beth felt tears coming to her eyes. But she was quickly in control of herself; this was no time to break down.

She said, "Do you have another gun? One I can use?"

Blake Durant shook his head. "I've never needed but one gun, ma'am. I don't expect I'll ever need another, not even tonight."

As he spoke he thought he heard a rumble of sound in the distance. He lifted his hand and motioned for her to be quiet. He listened intently for some time before she saw a nerve jump in his temple. Then he hurried to the horses, took some rope out of his saddlebag and hobbled them with it. Coming back, he signaled for her to get into the cover of two rocks.

When she was settled there, he took his position behind the saddles, lying flat, his gun pointed down the thin track they had come up.

* * *

Tom Carne swore as a prickly piece of brush cut his forearm. Then he studied the ridgeline above him. Chandler was close to him, out of the saddle and looking trail-weary and angry.

"Reckon they could climb all that today, Dan?" Carne asked. "The woman and him?"

Dan Chandler looked and shook his head doubtfully. "Hard to tell. Durant wants to get over as soon as possible, that's for sure."

"Be a mile straight up," Carne grumbled. "We been climbin' three parts of the day and we're only two thirds up. And we're men."

Chandler was too tired to argue, although he suspected that Blake Durant was more of a man than Carne was ready to give him credit for being. He'd confronted Pullen and Woodrow as openly as if they were kids. Then he'd cut down Sylvester.

"If Durant and the girl made that height today in the one climb, the girl won't be going too far tonight," Chandler said.

But Carne was scarcely listening to him now. He walked away from Dan Chandler and looked over his men. What he saw were six men leaning against rocks, looking to have as much fight in them as rabbits.

He said, "We'll give it one more hour. Then we'll take a breather. Anybody wantin' to pull out on me?"

The men returned his savage look silently, then their heads began to go down. Carne nodded, satisfied, then he walked on, leading his horse. When he reached a broad part of the trail, he swung onto the leg-weary horse, pulled his hat down to shade his eyes, and kicked the horse on.

It was slow climbing now along a trail that twisted and turned constantly. Carne looked neither to the right nor left, his stare probing upwards, seeing the snake of a trail and hating it, hating the hard work, and the sweating. And hating Durant. He wondered what Durant looked like and realized he had never seen the man.

Blake Durant was a good opponent. Carne liked that. Lately there had been too many easy pickings. His men had gone soft. What they needed was some stiff opposition to bring out the best in them, to restore their confidence in themselves. He thought again of Dan Chandler and decided that Chandler was maybe an unsettling influence on the others. Since the night he had taken his beating from Ty Pullen, Chandler had taken on the air of a man scheming to get back his standing. Carne wouldn't let that happen.

It was quiet along the ridge trail as Carne stared moodily at the tracks ahead. It would soon be night and they'd have to stop. But he had the feeling that Durant and the girl were close by. Durant had tackled the mountain and that had been his first mistake. Once on the other side he'd have to cross open country, and he'd leave clear tracks. They'd catch him easy.

Carne found himself smiling. He was even beginning to like the hunt now. It had been a long time since he had been involved in anything of this sort.

He was close. He could feel it inside him. Dwarfed by the huge boulders on his left as the trail turned sharply, he moved like a ghost in a vast, empty world, wary of what lay ahead, but impatient to come to grips with it.

Carne stopped to let his horse step over a rock planted in the middle of the trail. He looked down, where broken country stretched for many miles. There were trees and grass down there, but up here only gravel and rock.

Chandler drew up beside him, looking at him as though expecting Carne to say they'd stop. Carne read his thoughts and shook his head.

"Not yet, Dan. Couple of hundred feet up there where the trail broadens out—that'll be a good place for the men to stretch their legs."

Chandler kicked his horse ahead of Carne's and took up the lead.

The trail became more difficult to negotiate in the failing light, but Dan Chandler had no thought of stopping. He would not give Carne the satisfaction of ordering him to continue, but soon they must all stop or somebody would go over the side. Carne realized this, Chandler knew; it was his stubbornness that wouldn't let him call a halt.

So, brooding, Chandler kept his horse going. Only when the trail finally broadened did he draw rein. He sat there wiping his brow with a bandanna.

Carne rode up to Chandler and gradually the rest of the bone-weary group gathered around them. Before them for fifty feet or so, the ground was level. Carne eyed the place speculatively for a long time before he grunted in satisfaction and said:

"Spread out and bed down. We'll be headin' on before sunup. Eat and then get some rest. I don't want no horsin' around or talkin' or grumblin'."

Tom Carne came out of the saddle and pushed his horse away. The men filed past him and he studied each in turn, knowing their names, knowing who were the best in a pinch, knowing whom he could trust to kill and go on killing. He gave Chandler the benefit of the longest scrutiny. If Chandler was aware of it, his face showed no sign.

Then the first shot came, taking all of them by surprise. Carne, not stirring from the rock he was sitting on, drew his gun.

His black eyes narrowed as he saw one of his men grab at his shoulder. A second shot sounded and another gun hand fell clutching at his kneecap.

Then Dan Chandler went forward, bent over, gun out, and Carne made to go after him. But a barrage of shots came down at them from a cluster of rocks. Carne couldn't make out what it was, but he pumped off four shots before he crossed to where Dan Chandler knelt.

Carne said, "Be him all right, Dan."

"Who else?" said Chandler and he went down on his stomach and rammed shells into his gun. The two wounded men had gone past them, one dragging his ruined leg, and the other four had flattened themselves on the rocky ground. Silence settled after the rolling echo of the shots died in the distance.

A full minute passed before Carne told Chandler to go forward and try to get behind the rock cluster. Chandler gave him a sullen look as he rose to his elbows. The light was rapidly failing but it was still strong enough for the man above to see him clearly.

Chandler finally got to his knees. As he began to straighten, the sweat dripping from his jaw, another shot sounded. Chandler let out a howl of rage and pain and fell back, on top of Carne, who cursed, heaved him away and rolled to the side. His gun bucked and six shots tore into the barricade of rocks.

The rest of the men triggered bullets into the same target and for minutes the whole ridgeline rocked with the gunfire.

Then Carne called a halt to the shooting. He could see the huge bulk of Chandler lying only a few feet away. He called out, "Dan, you okay?"

There was no answer.

"Chandler, damn you!" Carne snapped. "You hurt bad or not?"

Again there was silence. Cass Bailey worked across to Chandler. After a short time he said, "He's gone, Tom. Got one clean through the head."

Carne sucked in a quick breath and began to crawl back down the slope. The others, not waiting for a direction, followed his example. When they were all together and Carne was squatted in the cover of a boulder, he said:

"Who was them others who got hit?"

Bailey went off to find out and came back looking as sullen as Carne had ever seen him. That pleased him. He liked to see fight in a man.

"Petersen got it in the knee and can't walk a step. Bocker's shoulder's been torn out. He's unconscious but not dead."

Bocker and Petersen were two good men. Now that that fool Chandler was out of the way, it left only Cass Bailey, the Willis boys and Ben Atcheson. Durant had sure won this round. And, positioned as he was above them, he would have the advantage in the morning, too—if he decided to remain there. Tom Carne was going to find that out right away.

"Cass, just as soon as it's dark take Ben with you and go down below aways and see if you can't climb up another way and get behind them. Take your time and be real careful. Be enough light if you go slow and feel your way. If you can get to the top of that ridge, by hell we'll have them right where we want them."

Cass Bailey gave Carne a guarded look which Carne ignored. But Ben Atcheson, who was an awkward man at the best of times, muttered, "Why don't we all wait till morning? Be easier and safer climbing by then."

"We wait, Durant might get a night's start on us, Ben. Now don't fret. Ain't nobody gonna get hurt, less'n it's a spook waitin' out there in them rocks."

Ben Atcheson studied Cass Bailey as if hoping he would put in a protest. But Bailey was silent, staring down the trail. The quiet became deeper until only the whisper of the wind disturbed it.

* * *

Blake Durant refilled his gun and edged back from the barricade. He found Beth Matheson looking at him with horror in her face. He ignored her and rummaged around in his saddlebag for a fresh carton of shells which he slowly proceeded to prod into the empty holes in his gunbelt. Beth couldn't take her eyes off him. He looked so calm.

Finally she could stand it no longer and said in a hoarse whisper, "You killed three of them. Three men."

"I didn't," Durant said. "I wounded two of them to slow them down. The third was meaning to come up here so I had to stop him."

"It's not that I think you didn't have to fight, Mr. Durant," she said in a strangely modulated voice. "But you just lay there and then you waited until they exposed themselves so you could shoot them down. Surely that makes you no better than they are."

Blake looked curiously at her. "Maybe I should have let them reach us," he said angrily. "Would that have suited you better?"

"They didn't all kill my husband and my nephew, Mr. Durant," Beth said. "It's Carne I want to see die. Surely the others are not to blame for—"

"Ma'am," Blake said wearily, "that outfit is packed with no-good killers. They raided your place and killed your husband and nephew. Then they proceeded to burn you out."

"But that was because Paul did something they didn't like. It must have been that. Perhaps he betrayed them."

"There was another ranch house burned in that area," Blake told her. "And likely more people were killed. I didn't have time to check it out on my way to Sage Creek, but it looks to me as if Carne and his outfit are trying to take over the whole territory. So just be quiet."

Beth sat back from him. When he had fired the shots, his eyes had been cold, vacant. He had killed without feeling, and possibly he'd even liked doing it. So whatever tenderness she might have felt for him was gone now.

Durant crawled back to the saddles and began removing the rocks from around them. Then he pulled the saddles free, one at a time, and packed them on the top of the boulder she was resting against. Beth's eyes followed his every move. She watched him tie pads made of blanket strips to the hoofs of the horses. Then, when he stood over her with his hands stretched down to help her up, she said:

"I'll manage."

"Suit yourself, Mrs. Matheson. But listen to me now and listen good. We're going on. Not far. Before darkness set in I noticed another clearing like this with perhaps as much cover. Carne won't, unless he's completely loco, make another attack tonight. He'll realize I have all the advantages. But in the morning, he'll come like a crazy man. By then I hope to have you over the rim and down the other side."

"On my own?" she asked, terrified again. The shock of the fight was beginning to wear off. It seemed that everything around her was brutal and vicious and evil. Even Durant.

"I'll try to link up with you later," he said. "If I don't make it, just press on. But for now take my provisions and pack them in your saddlebags. There's enough for one person for five days, taking care."

Beth regarded him curiously. "Is that all the food we have left?"

"It's enough. Once Carne is stopped I can shoot some game or catch some fish. Also, there's the likelihood of running into a ranch house."

Beth watched him open the saddlebags for her to remove the provisions. Hardly thinking what she was doing, she moved back as Durant leaned down and lifted both saddles to his shoulders, carefully catching the leather and irons in his hands. He then told her to bring the horses.

With Durant leading, they turned out of their cover and started the slow ascent to the top of the rim. From time to time Durant stopped and made her remain quiet while he listened. But there was no sound but the swish of the wind and the faint thuds of their boots on the rocky ground.

CHAPTER NINE
Impatience Unreined

Tom Carne looked bleakly at Cass Bailey as Bailey crawled back into the clearing. He knew from the expression on Bailey's face that something had gone wrong.

He asked, "Where's Atcheson, Cass?"

"Gone," Bailey said tightly.

"Gone? Gone where?"

Bailey shook his head. "I wondered why he took his horse down with him. When I said to leave it behind, he didn't answer me—he just went on, leading it. About three hundred yards down, he got onto the horse and told me to go to hell. He said to tell you that he's through with you."

Carne leaped to his feet, his face bloated with anger. He reached out and grabbed Cass Bailey by the neck and forced him to his knees with a choking grip. Then he held his gun to Bailey's mouth and snarled:

"You let him go, damn you! You let him run out on me!"

Bailey shook his head. "No, Tom. He had a gun on me. He wasn't taking any chances. Before I could try to stop him he was gone."

Carne's heavy breathing broke the night's stillness. The Willis brothers, Kip and Lyle, sat watching nervously.

Like Atcheson they had been thinking of pulling out. As they saw it, this was a fool trip into mountain country, with no real rewards to come out of it. Carne's fight was with Durant, and they were beginning to doubt if Carne would win out, with or without them.

Carne finally shoved Bailey away from him and paced up and down the clearing. In the darkness, his footsteps sounded clear and loud but he didn't seem to care about the danger of being shot down. Pullen was dead. So were Woodrow, the fool, and Dan Chandler. And now Ben Atcheson had cut out. That left him with Bailey, the Willis boys and two wounded men.

He stopped pacing suddenly and cocked his ear as if listening for a sound. But after a moment's concentration, he shrugged and came back to squat near the others.

"Nobody else moves out," he said and his stare swept over each face. When no one spoke, he went on, "At first light we'll be up and after Durant. Tomorrow we'll get him. I don't care if we've got to crawl on our knees—tomorrow that drifter gets his and he gets it hard."

Carne started to breathe heavily again but the others didn't seem to be listening. Each man sat looking down at the ground, each with his own thoughts and each with his own fear. Tom Carne paced up and down, cursing or just muttering. He kept it up all through the night so that none of the others got any sleep at all, and when the first gray light of day crept in through the brush, he was standing stock-still at the clearing's edge, looking up.

Cass Bailey made a smokeless fire and put on coffee as the Willis brothers squatted near him watching the flames lick about the sides of the old pot. When Carne was out of hearing, Lyle Willis, the older of the brothers, said:

"What do you figure, Cass?"

Cass Bailey looked at him through bloodshot eyes. He was so tired he didn't think he could ride a mile. "About what, Lyle?"

"Tom walkin' all night. Strikes me he aims to go through hell to get Durant."

"Seems like," put in his brother Kip, a brash youth who was one of the fastest guns in the outfit but who lacked the fire of the rest of them.

Bailey swung his look onto Kip Willis. He had never had much to do with either of the Willis boys, who usually kept to themselves. But they were good men in a fight.

"Yeah, he'll go through hell all right, Lyle," Bailey said.

"And take us with him, Cass. We'll have no chance going up there. Durant would just cut us down."

Cass Bailey licked his lips and cast a quick glance over his shoulder. Carne was walking back to them, his back straight and his gun swinging at his right side.

"Tell it to the boss man," Bailey said and rose from the fire to rub his eyes.

Carne squatted down, poured himself a mug of coffee and sipped. The others might not have been there, so absorbed was he in the movements of the flames about the pot. Finally he finished his coffee and tossed the mug aside. Then he stood, pulled his gunbelt higher on his waist and said:

"I think he's moved on."

Relief showed in Lyle Willis' face and Carne's stare narrowed on the tall, lean gun hand.

"But he ain't goin' too far, not with us stayin' right on his trail. Now you all had a good night's rest so there's no reason for anybody to drag behind. We'll all keep together, right up front, and when we run into Durant, we'll go straight for him and take our chances."

"What if he's behind cover?" put in Kip Willis.

"Then we go over the cover, mister, clean over."

Kip shrugged and came to his feet. He wiped the coffee stains off his mouth, took out his gun and checked it. When he looked at Tom Carne he smiled.

Carne frowned.

But Kip Willis merely said, "You ready to go, Mr. Carne?"

Carne licked his lips and screwed his mouth around. He wasn't sure of Kip Willis. But Pullen had told him that he'd ride anywhere with either of the Willis boys. At the time that had been enough for Tom Carne. But, up here, when somebody was sure to be killed trying to get to Durant, he wasn't so confident.

"Sure, I'm ready, Willis," Carne said. "I've been ready all damned night. Get your horses."

Carne kicked dirt over the small fire and then booted the coffee pot down the slope. Disregarding the scowling look on the face of Lyle Willis who owned the coffee pot, Carne brought his horse out of cover and swung onto it. He didn't wait for the others to bunch but rode on. He went straight up to the defense position Durant had used the previous evening and smiled broadly.

"Smart," he said to himself. "Real smart and fancy."

Then he looked back and saw the Willis brothers coming up the trail together, Bailey following. The wounded pair hadn't made a sound that morning and Carne hadn't even bothered to check on them.

When the others arrived he pointed to the ground and said with a grin, "See how clever our fancy jasper is. Padded his horses' hoofs and made off silently. Guess by now he's put some good twenty miles between him and us. So we'd best get movin' to pick up the leeway. First to see him gets a hundred extra out of our next haul."

With that Tom Carne, relaxed despite lack of sleep, pushed his horse up the trail.

* * *

Beth Matheson didn't sleep a wink during the night. Nor did Blake Durant. He sat opposite her after saddling her horse and stared moodily at the ground between his boots. Only once had she been tempted to speak, to ask him what he thought their chances were, but she had decided against it. So the night had passed in silence, while she tried to remember how badly she had behaved towards him after the Carne attack. She knew she had called him a killer and she felt sorry for this, but surely he must have known how shocked she was, not having been through an experience of that sort in her life. She doubted if she would ever forget the sight of that man dying or the calmness of Blake Durant.

Now, with the night dying, she saw that Blake was asleep. She was astounded by this, and thoroughly shocked when suddenly, as if alarmed, he came awake. He looked at her, then stared about him at the sky and said:

"Time you were going, Mrs. Matheson."

"All right," she said. She walked straight across to her horse and climbed into the saddle. Everything was ready for her departure and nothing should have delayed her. Yet she sat there, looking down at him and feeling a strange warmth flowing through her.

"Last night I said some things," she said.

"You were tired and worried, and maybe shocked."

"Yes, I was shocked, terribly so."

"Some things are hard to live through. No matter how many times you see a man die, it's hard to get used to. No matter how bad he was either—he was once a living, breathing thing and suddenly he knows no more."

"Then you do feel something," she said. "I ... I thought ..."

"You thought I didn't care," he said with a faint smile. "I know that. You were wrong, but it doesn't matter."

"But it does matter, Mr. Durant," Beth said. "I wanted to like you and perhaps I hoped that one day I would love you. But this hasn't been the right time to let myself go. It's too soon and I'm too confused."

Blake walked across to her and smiled up warmly. "Mrs. Matheson, if it was meant to be, it would have been. Go on your way now and keep going. Late today, or perhaps tomorrow, I'll catch up. If not, I wish you luck."

"You will come," she said suddenly. "You must come."

"Perhaps."

Beth leaned down and kissed him on the lips. She let her mouth linger there, waiting for his response. When it didn't come she pulled back and frowned down at him. Blake turned her horse around and pointed the way out for her, then he stepped back and watched her go. He felt a deep sense of relief when he saw her go over the rim and out of sight. Immediately he pushed all thoughts of her out of his mind. Trouble was coming and he wanted a fresh mind so he could deal with it.

Beth had been gone only five minutes when Durant saw the vague shape of horse and rider come out of the trail's grayness. He settled down behind the cover of brush and watched him come on. He had no idea who the man was. Then three other shapes loomed up close behind the lead man. This was going to be a slaughter. He didn't like the taste of that in his mouth but he knew it was inevitable, just as it was inevitable that he should kill a man who drew on him in any town on the frontier. His own life and a woman's life were at stake, and perhaps the future of a town was in his hands.

The leading rider seemed to be looking at him. Blake saw the gun resting against the horse's shoulder and then he was able to make out the man's face. It was a face filled with hate. The others slowly came into focus and he recognized the runt from the saloon and two men who'd kept out of things when he'd confronted Pullen and Woodrow in the saloon. He had nothing against them.

But the front man was Carne, the killer who had come to Sage Creek territory to plunder, to terrorize, maim and kill. Blake had met his kind before.

Blake Durant took careful aim. He hated killing a man cold, but he was one against four who hunted him. He lifted the gun a fraction and punched off his first shot. The bullet tore into the nuggety little man's shoulder and plucked him from the saddle. The horse came on, neighing and slipping on the steep ridge trail. The other three men dropped from their saddles and ran for cover. For a few minutes Blake Durant kept his head down and listened to the buzz of bullets going past him.

When next he looked, Carne was only a few paces from him, crouched and glaring, heedless of the shoulder which poured blood down his sleeve and shirt front. Blake recognized the insane hatred in the contorted face. He saw the twisted lips and the savage light in his black eyes.

Blake showed himself to give Carne his chance. Carne went lower into his crouch. Then his gun began punching out shots. Blake fired at the same time and the air between them seemed to explode into fragments. Carne kept walking forward until his gun was empty. Then he stopped suddenly. The runt Bailey was coming up fast now, and one of his bullets nicked Blake in the shoulder. Blake swung to confront Bailey, fired and sent him slithering on his back down the slope.

Then Carne toppled forward, almost into Blake's arms. Blake shifted and let him fall, then he looked down at a body riddled with five bullets. Carne was still and Blake Durant knew he would not move again.

He turned to give his attention to the other two, but he couldn't see them. He heard the breaking of brush as a horse tore through it and then a voice called, "It's finished, Durant! It's over!"

Blake Durant didn't say anything in return. He couldn't even be sure if he would recognize the two men again if he ran across them.

"Carne wanted this, Durant, not us. We're pulling out and you can go on your way. We won't follow you."

"I don't care if you do, mister," was Blake's shouted answer.

"Well, we care, mister. We saw enough of you. We rode with Carne because we figured it was as good an outfit as any for our kind. But we had it wrong, my brother and me. We ain't his breed, so we're pulling out. You take the girl where you like."

Blake waited, listening as two horses went down the trail. He swung onto Sundown and walked the horse a short distance down that trail himself, ready for another fight if it came his way. But after he had gone a few hundred feet he stopped and saw them, two men riding together and another two trailing.

The two behind looked to be badly hurt. He knew then that it was really over.

Retracing his steps up the ridge trail, he was surprised to find Beth Matheson waiting for him at the top. She had tears in her eyes.

"You saw?" he said.

Beth nodded. "It was terrible, but not so terrible as the last time. Can a person get used to it?"

Durant shook his head. "Nobody gets used to it."

"Not even you, Mr. Durant."

"Especially not me, Mrs. Matheson. Let's go back."

"Back?"

"There's nothing to fear now. There's nobody left. Carne's dead and his outfit has been busted up. Nobody need know how it happened or why. But somebody will have to stir the Sage Creek people up and get them moving. You'll have to look after your affairs now."

"Yes," Beth said.

They rode from the mountain and Blake set an even pace across the prairie. That night they camped at the creek. Durant had a good fire going.

The leaping flames gave Beth confidence. She spoke of her early years as a wife, of all she had hoped for from marriage ...

But Blake Durant didn't speak one word about his past. Finally she decided she would have to come right out with it, and she could think of no better place than this, with just the two of them and the wide prairie and the creek. "Mr. Durant," she said, "I want to call you Blake. May I?"

"Sure."

"And you will call me Beth. It will have to be like that, won't it, later on?"

Durant did not speak for some time. When he did his voice was husky. "A lot has happened, Beth. But time will help, perhaps a lot of time, maybe only a short time. I don't know and you don't know."

"Can I hope then?"

"'We can all hope."

Beth lay back, still puzzled. Then the only possible explanation for his manner struck her. It came as something of a shock that she had not thought of it before.

"Was she very beautiful, Blake?"

"Yes."

"Young and beautiful and you loved her."

"I loved her."

"What happened? Can't you talk about it? Wouldn't it be better to tell somebody instead of keeping it bottled up inside yourself, letting it hurt you all the time?"

Blake was silent for a long time before he said, "Beth, it doesn't hurt inside. It's a hard thing to explain, but it's there and in a way I want it to stay there. I think one day it will go away of its own accord because something will replace it. But I'll always remember ... I won't ever be able to forget. But the pain will go."

Beth felt tears in her eyes. She didn't know how to ask him the next question. She didn't have the nerve to do it, because she feared the answer. So she turned over and went to sleep and when she awoke in the morning, Blake Durant was still sleeping soundly. Beth rose, saddled her horse and minutes later she rode out of the camp. But she left her tears with him, and a note. If he wanted her, he could go after her. It was the only way she would ever be sure of knowing.

She rode through the day, feeling terribly lonely. Blake Durant didn't come after her. She remembered everything he'd said. He'd stared into her eyes when he'd said somebody would have to shake up some spirit in the people of Sage Creek. Now she sensed that he'd been referring to her.

She turned about and looked back, but the prairie was empty. She realized that for all her stealth, Blake Durant hadn't been asleep. It was his habit to be up early, and the slightest sound would have awakened him. He'd deliberately let her go.

Tears ran down her cheeks as she pictured him riding the other way, a strange and lonely man, the only person in her life who had, without hope of reward, helped her.

Well, that was settled. "I'll do it, Blake," she said. "I'll shake them up."

And Beth Matheson, widow, went on her way.